Petunia's Freight Night with Fred

Erin Lee
Rena Marin

Petunia's
Freight Night
with
Fred
INTERNATIONAL BESTSELLING AUTHORS
ERIN LEE
RENA MARIN

Publisher's Note: This is a work of fiction. Names, characters, places, and incidents are a product of the author's imagination. Locales and public names are sometimes used for atmospheric purposes. Any resemblance to actual people, living or dead, or to businesses, companies, events, institutions, or locales is completely coincidental.

Dedication

For anyone who's ever had a Freddy in his/her life.

Petunia in a mood

It doesn't matter *what* I say or do. Petunia isn't having it. It has been two full days since she's even eaten. While I *could* just shrug it off—it isn't like silicone brides have to pack it down to survive—I will not. No. Petunia is better than this. *My* Petunia is polite. In the old days, when she was first unboxed, she would never make such a fuss. But we aren't there now. And this isn't the first time. *That*, was the Fourth of July.

I glare at her, trying to determine why, exactly, she's so intent on making our harvest celebration so impossibly awkward. There's no way I'll be able to bring her to my mother's for a first introduction this year at Thanksgiving if she's going to act this way. It will be hard enough explaining that all the pictures they've seen are really of a plastic wife. But for her to have a pout on through a meal that took me two days to make? No. It can't be a thing. I'll never hear the end of it.

My best guess is that Petunia doesn't like sharing me. While I know she's uncomfortable with Renee and the rest of the wedding guests, she only seems to get like this when they are around. Maybe she's just jealous. I must admit, if that is it, I can't say I hate it. I wanted her to have a jealous streak. To me? Well, that's love.

But that can't be it. It isn't like she doesn't know they're part of the family. For goodness sake, it's not like they're new either. The guests have been around for almost a year now. There is no reason for her to be acting like this with only her immediate family. What the hell *will* my mother think if she's this impossibly rude?

"Petunia, Fred is waiting on you," I say, pulling the spoon closer to her mouth.

I can't possibly get to the other guests if Petunia won't swallow her meal down. It's true. I always feed her first. But we'll be here all night, under the gazebo, if she doesn't suck it up. It's getting cold. Hell, it's October in Vermont.

Yeah, I could move on to Fred or even Sylvia. But that isn't the point. The point is that I can be as stubborn as my bride. I've given her exactly everything. All I ask is she be the lady I created her to be. Lately, that seems more and more complicated. Between her newfound interest in being on the screen and some crazy idea she has about being a star to help with the cash flow around here, Petunia has lost not only her modesty but, apparently, her manners too. Worse, she's jealous over Fred's new talking chip. How the hell was I supposed to play poker with the dude without knowing whether or not he was all in or folding? It wasn't like she hadn't had help from Sage either. Petunia could be impossible to satisfy. *Entirely rude, too.*

Finally, I snap. "What is her **problem**, Brenda?"

Busty Brenda has served as the perfect, beautiful-but-don't-tell-Petunia, translator for us since our honeymoon in the Tennessee smoky mountains. Adding her to the family was one of the best decisions I made since unboxing my love. Had Petunia not stolen the talking chip and I'd skipped on the 'O', we'd probably have no problems at all right now. Instead, with my wife's limited ability to speak and her incessant requests for batteries, here we are.

Busty Brenda smiles at me and tilt's her head in Petunia's direction. Then, with the low hum of gears turning, she says, "She hates Fred."

"She hates Fred? Since when?"

"Since forever," Busty Brenda says.

"Why?" I don't know whether to believe her or if this is another of their stupid 'fuck with Guy' games.

I look over at Fred, who is positioned innocently enough at the other end of the outdoor lawn table waiting for me to come feed him. Who in the hell hates Fred? He's my best friend. The guy is the only one I can trust to listen to my marital problems. Hell, he wasn't even mad when I came home with a five-inch dong and attached it to him with no hope for more or apology either. Had I been in his position, I'd *still* resent him. *Average is as good as any other guy living under this roof gets.*

"Not sure. She just says he creeps her out. Guy? I'm hungry. When's my turn?"

I sigh. We will be here all night. Brenda has a point. If Petunia won't eat and we all wait on her no one will ever get fed.

"I'm feeding Fred first and you next," I say, standing and dragging my chair away from Petunia's to the other side of the table. I don't even look at her. I'm livid. We can finish this argument alone in the bedroom.

"Yay!" Brenda squeals like she's just won a prize at a carnival. She doesn't even notice my love hissing at her.

"Hey, bud," I say, reaching Petunia's spoon into Fred's plate. "Open up."

"See how his mouth hangs? That. That's why he freaks her out," Brenda says, entirely missing the point that I'm no longer interested in the topic.

I can't help it. It just falls out of my mouth as Brenda rambles on about how Petunia thinks Fred's funny looking and that real men aren't four feet tall. I say, "Bros before hos," and shove a mountain of mashed potatoes with chicken gravy into my silicone buddy's mouth.

Petunia's mouth hangs open.

I laugh out loud.

"Bros before hos," I say it again and turn back to Fred, tapping him on the shoulder.

I'm not sorry. In a way, since getting the 'O' Chip and cameras, she is a ho. She's always the first in line to be the star of the show. What I could do with other members of the family, she insists I use her for. Hell, she won't even let me film a scene with Renee and Fred. It's like she'd be scared or something if I took Fred's cock out. I'm over it. I'm over her too. I ordered a lady, and I've got nothing more now than a jealous brat.

Fred chomps down the potatoes as I change the subject again. Now, I'm gunning for Petunia's soul.

"I was thinking tonight we could film something new. How would you feel about showing off to our male doll fans? I talked to Bob and he said that it's a growing trend. Soon, the men will be more popular than the women. What do you think, dude?"

Obviously Fred won't answer me the way I wish he would. *I need to get* him *the AI upgrade. Then it would be two against twenty.* Still, he nods and says, 'yes, he'd be into it.' It's good enough for now. Petunia has the limited chip and Busty came equipped with almost as much technology as Sage. While it'd taken me some exploring to find out how to turn it on—exploration I'd never tell Petunia about—at least I have her for translation. Problem is she always takes my love's side. My home is becoming like a bad episode of Gender Wars.

I want to hit Fred in the back of the head and make him tell me more. His speech is okay at best, but his intelligence? Still far more limited than Brenda's. In that way, I am entirely outnumbered. If I want to piss Petunia off, I have to push him.

"You could be a star. Freddy the Fiend," I say.

"*I'm* the star!" Petunia squeals.

I pretend I don't hear her.

"Women love men like you, bud. It'll be fantastic. Here. Eat up. We have a big show tonight, and I just know you can pull it off."

I laugh as my buddy chomps down his entire plate. I ignore Brenda and even my love's two-word pleas. And, when his meal is complete, I move to Sylvia. Petunia and her bestie can hate me. Fred isn't creepy. And it's true. Sometimes, a guy's gotta put his friends first. Guy Code. That simple. I wonder if Bob has a chip for that too…

"Men love guys like you too," I tell Fred, raising my eyebrows and smiling at Petunia. Maybe, next time, she'll just fucking eat. Payback for ruining the family harvest dinner. I'm not sorry. Why should I be?

Petunia in frustration

Me, a ho? I don't think so. Fred has to go. There's no way around it, no way to deny, and no way I'm letting it go. I get it: Guy needs a friend. He can order another one. One that isn't so weird. He thinks I'm being crazy and has gone to the extent of calling me a brat several times lately, but he doesn't see the things I do. He doesn't understand Fred like I do. He's a creep. He's rude. He's a prick. And by hell, they can call me crazy all they want, but the stumpy man doll is obsessed with me.

I see the way he watches me. It weirds me out. I'll catch him staring from across the room, mouth moving like he wants to talk but nothing coming out. I often wonder if he has the hots for me, but I'm not sure if that's it. Maybe his new cock has catapulted him from annoying to pervert. I don't know, but there's something I just can't seem to put my finger on. Maybe Bob did more for him than any of us know.

It could be jealousy. I won't deny the streak that runs through me. I own that shit. I always have. Having the family around does take from our alone time. Guy doesn't seem to mind so much anymore though. And yes, I'm not calling him my love right now because he is being an asshole. When he stops, that may change. Until then, he's my husband, who's a dumbass.

I thought things would be different. Yes, I realize my calling. I'm to be on the screen, making those curious about my kind fall in love with me. I assume he will understand that, help me reach this goal, and be supportive. Nope. All he can think about is doing new things, with new dolls, and gaining more followers. Great. More dolls. As if having so many members of the family around isn't enough, he invites more.

I try to overlook all of them. Hell, poor Shelia often ends up forgotten since the new, silver-haired, Sylvia arrived. She is another gift from Bob. Of course, she isn't as advanced as Brenda, who is up there with Sage, but she is smarter than Fred; she just can't talk as much. Her limited vocabulary doesn't change the fact that she is engineered to be a bedroom goddess, or at least that's what her box had written on it. Her mouth is in a resting circle, obviously for doing naught things with a pecker. Most of the time she reminds me of those blow-up dolls the rival channels show. Her boobs aren't as big as Brenda's, thank God, but from what I understand, according to the conversations my husband has with Fred, her hoohah must be lined in gold. I've heard them talk about it being one helluva puss.

Maybe that's my problem with Fred. I get it. Guys will be guys. Even my Guy. But to hear him talk about other women, it doesn't exactly sit well with me. He doesn't seem to understand that it bothers me. Yes, he tries to keep the chatter away from my ears. It doesn't work though. At night when they are playing poker, laughing, smoking up the house with those nasty cigars, and getting drunk, I hear the talk. Just because I'm lying in bed, doesn't mean I'm asleep. Hell, even our sex life has suffered. I've found myself needing the vibrator more since Fred's chip than ever. Thank goodness, the all-powerful Bob, sent one that can be set on a timer. If not, I'm sure Guy would leave me upstairs overdosing on orgasms while he and Fred talk of Sylvia's perfect hoohah, Brenda's tits, and how Renee's new nipples are the bomb.

I guess I am outdated. My hoohah isn't anything special. My bosom isn't of the magnitude of Brenda's, and even poor, forgotten Shelia has prettier hair. Yes, I used to think I was the shit, but lately, I'm realizing maybe I'm not. Sure, I get comments on the videos I'm in. I have a few fans; one even used my name for his screenname, Petunialover69. Guy talks about blocking him, especially in the beginning he did, but Brenda talks him out of it. He shares a lot of our stuff. Those shares will help us get noticed. When she explains that point of view, Guy leaves it be. It doesn't bother him anymore. I guess he doesn't mind if I have a stalker.

I will admit, I've done things on camera I would've never imagined myself doing in front of others. The fame monster is alive and well within me. It isn't for me that I do it though. I know how much we're struggling. We need the cash. I want to help. This is the only way I can. It's not like I can go get a job at Wal-Mart or anything. Touching Brenda's big knockers seems to be one of the things the people on the channel like. Of course, we don't show her tits but they get a real kick out of my hand resting on those enormous things, and Guy acting like I did it myself. I'm not as lucky as the others though. He moves me around still. I'm fighting the cancer. I'm fighting hard. I just haven't won yet.

The video of me orgasming is our most liked one. That one was taken upstairs in our room. Brenda was there. With her AI intelligence, she was talking, kind of like coaching me, while Guy is off camera doing things with his hand to get me to that point. The oohs and moans must really fuck with people. The comments are insane. They are talking about bringing me home with them and how they could make me scream. There are comments I'd expect my husband to be angry about. He in't. He cracks up and shows them to Fred.

I'm not the only one in the house with the ability to get off. In the beginning, that video was going to be for Sylvia. There is no way in hell I am going to let Guy get her off. Nope. He tries to convince me it is all for the channel. No buddy, I know better. It is your chance to play with the golden cunt and go brag to Fred about it. Not happening. I may be losing my husband to Fred, which is bad enough, but I will be damned if I'm going to sit around and wonder if he is thinking about Sylvia and her porno pussy while he is with me. My vibrator is enough of an issue in our bedroom; we don't need her in there too.

I see Brenda giving me a look. I know what she wants me to do. She would prefer I eat, stop giving Guy shit, and let go of my issues with Fred. She isn't married, so I guess she doesn't understand how hard that is for me. My husband is across the table, feeding Fred, and talking about the video they will be making tonight. I'm sure it will be something kinky and get everyone going on and on about Fred and his little pecker. Great. That means he'll be sticking around.

***

By the time dinner is finished and the table cleared up, I'm in my chair while Guy is busy taking the others where he wants them. Like I figured, Sylvia and Fred are in the living room while the others have been shuttled away to wherever he has them stashed. Poor Renee, I bet she's jealous as hell. I'm not a fan of Fred, so I have no reason to stay. Luckily, my limited capabilities do allow me to yawn. Maybe that will convince him to take me upstairs, so I don't have to witness Freddy the Fiend. It should be named Freddy the Fucktard.

"Petunia is tired," I hear Brenda announce.

I do love her. She is the best friend a girl can have. I may not be able to tell these asshats what I'm thinking, but she gets me. She also doesn't mind arguing with Guy. She's great at it. The two of them have been known to go full force for well over an hour. She doesn't like not getting the last word in. I guess it's a girl thing.

Clearly annoyed, Guy leaves Fred where he is on the couch, then says he'll get things ready for me. Good. Thank you. Your wife appreciates the fact you are providing her with a few spare moments of your precious time. Ugh!

Hearing him stomp up the stairs, I look over at Brenda. She's just as shocked as I am. It's nice to have someone who understands what you're going through. She doesn't get Guy's new obsession with the others either. She says I'm still the sweetest thing she's ever met. I'm glad she'll always have my back. Guy should take note though. I love Brenda; she's my girl, but I don't put her before him. No onewill hear me screaming "chicks before dicks" or anything.

Wondering what he's doing in our room that is taking so much time, I yawn again, wishing he was down here to see my frustration. I'm sure Fred will tell him all about it though. Brenda looks my way, giving me her best, 'I get it girl,' look. I smile until I see Fred's head turn in my direction.

What the actual hell? He isn't supposed to be able to do that. He has a voice chip and nothing more. His mouth moves. Not his fucking head. I look over, wondering if there were upgrades given to him my love hasn't bothered to tell me about. That's when I see it. He's smiling at me. It's strange though. It's not like the normal look Fred gives. No, something is off. Something is freaky.

"No," I say, wishing I could say more like "stop looking at me you, crazy bastard," but I can't.

In answer, his head slowly nods "yes," the insanely creepy grin still in place. I look over at Brenda, who isn't paying the least bit of attention to Fred. Before I can do anything to make her see what I see, his head returns to its normal position and the smile slowly changes to the dumbfounded look he's famous for. *What the hell just happened?* If Guy went and ordered Fred more shit, I'm going to come out of this chair and kick his ass. I need to know, though. If Guy didn't upgrade Fred behind my back, we may have a real problem here.

Petunia in jealous rage

Convinced I know what her issue is, I pull a U-turn and head right back down the stairs. I don't care if the family gets tucked in tonight. Frankly, it isn't my job to worry about the cousins. I do enough for them. I've taken on Petunia's plastic family as my own. I'm the best in-law in all of America. Hell, I spoon feed them. But tonight, finally aware of what her problem is, it's gonna be about me. Me and my buddy.

Taking the stairs two at a time, I don't even stop to look at her. Instead, I grab Fred under the under arms. "Come on, bud. Guys' night," I say, pulling his weight forward and bending at the knee to pull him into my arms.

I don't care if it takes me an hour. I refuse to retreat to the basement like normal. No. Tonight, and no matter how it appears to my love and her stupid girl squad, I'm sleeping with Fred. She can call me gay; she can tell me I'm playing for another team. She can run out of batteries and whine that I don't find her sexy anymore. Whatever. I simply don't care. I can already hear her and Busty Brenda saying, "bless him."

Fred doesn't argue with me. To my shock and relief, he simply melts into me as I lug him up the stairs, never looking back at my bride. She can run her own bath. She can sleep on the couch with the show squad talking about how I don't pay them enough. Christ, at this point, I don't care if she logs on and talks to PetuniaLover69 or whatever his name is. For tonight, just this one night, I'm teaching her a lesson. I'll deal with her in the morning. The consequences of it too.

It takes a full half hour to finally reach the crest of the stairs. There, against the stark white wall, I push Fred off of me and allow him to fall naturally back. Now, in a close-as-it-gets to standing position without the suspension rods, I smile at him.

"Sorry, dude. Chicks. Don't worry. She's just jealous that I have a friend. I'm over it. Over her too. It's our night. I'll get you set up, and we can play poker up here. No need to worry about them interrupting us either. Anything you want me to grab?"

"Cigars."

"Check."

"Chips?"

"You got it. Now, I'm going to slide you down on your side, so you don't fall."

"Good idea, Guy. And you're right. Fuck the girls. I'm sick of them too."

"Any time."

Gently, the same way I pulled my love out of the box and even how I lowered Sarah into the dirt, I bring Fred to the carpeted ground. There, I lay him on his side and tell him I won't be long.

***

An hour and two poker hands later

"I just don't get it, dude."

"Well, me either. She might be jealous of the new girl…"

"I don't care. She's jealous of you too. It's so stupid. I've done everything for her! It's not like I'm the type that turns a chick in for a new model. She should know better! I restored the house, basically gave up my job. Set up the channel. Hell, the only reason you and the others are here is so she could have the perfect family. Does she think it's *cheap* cooking for thirty every night? Is it *easy* giving a cheerleading team showers or baths every day? I hardly have time for anything! Let alone keeping Marcy away from me!"

"Technically, we don't have to eat," Fred says, staring down at his hand. I try to watch his eyes. Normally, when Fred has a full house, he blinks. Blinks twice for a royal flush. It's connected to the artificial intelligence from what I can see, but

I could be wrong. It's still new having a best guy friend to talk back and play with me.

"I wasn't raised that way. I mean, Petunia or not, this is *still* Gram's house. When I'm around and cooking, I can't not offer it up. She'd roll over in her grave."

Fred's expression changes. He hesitates, looks at me, and finally asks for a light. Pulling the lighter from my back pocket, I hook him up with a Cuban cigar and wait. Finally, "Where is Grams these days, anyway?"

I want to burst out laughing. Clearly, me and Petunia's secret about the bodies under the gazebo is no longer safe. Nothing in this house is. Not with the AI chips.

"Dude! Really? She's in Rolling Hills Cemetery. Just up the street. By the Westminster Congregational Church. Geesh."

"Well, you never know."

The shit Fred comes up with is a kick. I wonder, sometimes, if Petunia thinks the same things. "I would not bury Grams in the back yard," I say, knowing he probably doesn't believe me. Shit you not. Rolling Hills Cemetery. Harris & Son's Funeral Home took care of it all for me. I swear! Third plot in the new section to the left by the trees."

"But why not? If you buried her here, she could be with the rest of the family."

It is odd that he isn't judging me. Did plastic dolls think it was cool to shoot people's faces off for staring too long and taking pictures? Maybe it was the AI that is limiting? Is he aware of Sarah's moldy body and that, in theory, she'd done nothing more than use me? Is the guy a sociopath with no conscience at all? For a second, Fred scares me with the thought of it. *Busty Brenda said Petunia was freaked out by him. Thinks he's creepy. ...Naw. He just doesn't get it,* I think, pulling for a cigar of my own.

"It's different with people you love," I say. And then, just to make it clear, "I'm not that kind of man. Like, I have a conscience. What those officiants did to Petunia was over the top. And Sarah? She's another story for another day. Petunia doesn't like it when I even think about her, and she believes Sarah got what she deserved."

Why I'm justifying anything to a guy whose chip I could pull at any second is beyond me. But it matters to me what Fred thinks. Appearing satisfied, he throws down another buck.

"I'll raise you five," I say, hoping he doesn't have a full house like last time.

Fred nods, rubbing his forehead. Is it another tell or bluff? I have to give it to the guy. Sometimes, his expressions are out of line with what they might be for a normal guy. Fred is complicated. It's probably why he freaks Petunia out.

"For real, if you want, tomorrow we can visit Grams in the cemetery. She'd be excited to see I have a friend. I'm not ready yet for her to meet

Petunia. It could be like a trial run for Thanksgiving."

Fred is more than aware of how nervous I am about the upcoming holiday with my human family and silicone bride. It's been far too long and I've made way too many excuses for it to be believable anymore. They have to meet the girl I married someday.

Besides, if I wait much longer, my step brother is sure to stumble upon me and my love's channel. Last week, we went viral after Petunia and Busty Brenda put on a show to remember. Worse, with Sylvia in the house, well, it just won't be long. I need to tear the band aide off.

"You worry too much. I mean, they have to know. Petunia is outdated. You can see the lines where her neck connects to her head," Fred says, still staring at the cards in his hand, which tells me he has nothing. High key irritated that he's ripping on my love, I hope he tries to bluff.

"She can wear a turtle neck."

"Won't do it. Look at how she moves her head."

"I know they will know when we get *there*. It's not like they are Marcy. I can't steer her away from them. It will be kind of obvious when I'm feeding her mashed potatoes with gravy and my uncle's sausage stuffing that she's a doll. What I mean is that they can't tell *for now*. In the pictures I post, she appears totally human."

"Sure. If you say so. But here's what I wonder: Why do you care?"

The guy's got a point. I shouldn't care what my family thinks. My mother's been through enough men and failed relationships that she'd probably be better off with a guy like Fred too. Had she not told me to move Sarah in to Grams' house to help me take care of her, hell, things might even be different for me. I might have met a human woman and not even have this issue. But shit works out how it's supposed to.

"You're probably right. They are just so judgmental."

Fred shrugs, pulling at his cigar, turning his head, and letting out a huge puff of sweet smoke. "So judge um back. With the way the channel's going? Shit. You and Petunia are about to be stars. Soon, your mom will be all over you for cash."

He wasn't wrong there either. My mother and the rest of my family had a way of showing up when they needed something. Maybe, me and Petunia should just bail on Thanksgiving dinner—again—all together. They could find out on the channel—if they hit subscribe and paid the monthly 10.99. It was a thought… With the family harvest dinner over and done, why did we really need another one?

Petunia in preparation

He left me here? He actually *left* me sitting here to go spend the night with Freaky Fred! What the actual hell is he thinking? In all my days, yes there aren't that many of them, but I'm no spring chicken, I have never been treated this way. Even the asses at the warehouse, my friend Rena excluded of course, didn't treat me this way. They covered me each night when it got dark and saw to dusting me daily. Now, because of Fred, I can't even go to my own bed or have a decent bath, *in my own home*! What is Guy thinking?

"We will make the best of it," Brenda tells me from her position on the couch beside me.

I want to go off and tell her I will not put up with this kind of treatment, but what can I do? I'm not the rest of them. I can't say exactly how I'm feeling. All I can really do is say a couple of normal daily phrases and my name. I can't say "suck my ass till the cows come home, love," to my husband like I want to. Nope. He has me on this one.

"Fred is trying to take over," Brenda continues as her head slowly turns to look at me. "He doesn't like you."

"I know," I tell her in agreement. She's right though. I figured that part out already. Something about Fred doesn't sit well with me, and he feels the exact same way. Hell, if he had *his* way, I'd probably be out in the backyard with the corpses instead of inside with my husband and family. He's most likely rooting for the cancer to come out of remission. Asshole.

I can hear the two of them upstairs talking. I can't make out the exact conversation or anything, my hearing isn't as good as the others, but it's easy to tell they are having a good time. In my room!

I may never sleep in that bed again. Knowing that Fred is up there, doing whatever, with my husband infuriates me. If I had the means, I'd march my ass right out the front door and leave Guy worrying about where I went. I don't, of course, so that will never be an issue, but still, giving him something to worry on would be nice. He's able to walk out and leave me. I have to sit here and deal with his bullshit.

"We can have a girl's night."

I look over at Brenda. Bless her heart; she is trying her best to keep me from being upset. She's such a great friend. I wish Guy had invited her over for the wedding instead of all the others. I know that sounds bad considering they're my cousins and all that, but they don't get me like Brenda. Fred isn't family. I don't care what Guy says. He can holler "Fred is so-and-so to me," but in my book, he ain't shit.

"I can't wait," I tell Brenda. It's the best I can do with my voice still on the mend. She understands though. She's never been upset about my limited capabilities or the havoc the cancer has reeked on me. Instead, she tries to console me through it. See why I like her?

"Fred has a little dick," she says abruptly.

I don't know how to take what she's just said. I laugh, of course, who wouldn't when faced with an asshole's small penis size, but I can't help but wonder why it's important information.

"I think he's jealous of you and Guy. I don't know if he likes Guy in that way or just wants you out of the way to spend more time with him. It could be penis envy though. He may be upset Guy's is bigger. At least, I think it's bigger," she smirks.

I laugh again. "Yes, bigger," I answer wishing I could have a full conversation with her. I'd demonstrate with my hands the size and all that like girls do in the movies. I can't though. One day, when I'm better I will. It's not like I'm going to tell her to give it a try and find out either. Nope, not happening. I love her, but with those tits, I'd never see my husband again.

"See, Fred wants Guy's life. He wants to be the big penis of the house."

Could she be right? Is that the game Fred is playing? Is he cozying up to my husband in hopes of taking Guy's place around here? I guess it could be possible, but how would that work? Fred can't cook. Fred can't make videos. Fred damn sure isn't hopping in our bed with me. Then again, he wouldn't have to would he? No, my husband, who is bright as a burned-out lightbulb, has brought several females into this house Fred could claim as his bride. All he would need to do is get me and Guy out of the way. Then he'd have the run of the place, and like Brenda said, be the head dick in charge.

"We're smarter, though."

She's right on that one. In no way is Fred more intelligent than me and Brenda. I may be southern, but all that bullshit about us being dumb is for the birds. I have a brain. I use it. I may not be able to say what is on my mind, but that doesn't mean I'm a dumbass. I'm no inbred yokel who runs around screaming the south will rise again or anything, but I do take pride in where I'm from. Maybe that southern ingenuity and downhome charm is what I need right now. I'm Petunia. I can charm the pants off anyone.

"Yes, we are." I agree knowing Brenda will see the gleam in my eye.

"You need to get Guy back on our side," she continues. "You're his wife. Make him remember how much better you are than Fred."

I sigh. That's the hard part. I love Guy. He is my whole world, but lately, I haven't been his. "That's the hard part," I tell her knowing she'll understand where I'm coming from.

"No, it's not. You have something Fred doesn't have," she tells me, then winks. "A vagina."

I stare at her. I know the look on my face gives me away thanks to the laughter that ensues. Surely, she isn't telling me to show my hoohah off around the house. It damn sure won't compare to the golden cunt down the hall, and I have more manners than that.

"Explain," I ask hoping she isn't thinking of turning me into a whore. I can't do that. Yes, I do things for the channel I wouldn't normally do, but that's for the audience, and the money we need so bad.

"Win Guy over with what you have to offer. Get him back on your side. Make him forget Fred," she tells me with a shake of her head. "You forget, Petunia, you're the one he is in love with. Make him remember that."

She's right. Guy is my husband, not Fred's. Or at least I hope that's still the case. I don't know what the two of them may end up doing up there, alone in my room. With the mouth on Fred, he may give a helluva blowjob, I have no idea. Still, Brenda has a point. If I can get Guy to notice me again, maybe Fred will fade away. I can be his Fred. I can be his friend, talk shit about people, and even learn to play poker. I may need help until I'm completely better, but Brenda is always here for that. If I make myself Guy's best friend, and the perfect lover, he'll have no more use for Fred, and he can find his way out into the graveyard out back. Or we could send him back to Bob, but I like the burying him idea better. Either way, I'd win, which is how it should be. Now, I need a plan.

"I'll help you."

I smile over at Brenda. I knew she'd be in this with me. I suppose its going to be the perfect boys vs. girls, thing. We're smarter though. And I'm damn sure better equipped.

"You need to use those perky tits."

I nodded in agreement.

"You need to pucker those lips and bat those eyes."

Check, I can do that.

"You need to give him the best sex ever. In the mood or not. No more vibrator."

Damn. I hate saying goodbye to my little friend, but if it means getting Freaky Fred out of my life, I'll do it. Check.

"Then, when Fred is gone, we work on getting you fixed up. You should be the one running this house. Not Fred. And not Guy."

You know, she's right. I'm the lady of the house. This should by my show, not theirs. Sure, Guy is my husband and my partner, but it's time I took my rightful place as the lady of this dollhouse. Game over, Fred. Petunia is about to show you how a true southern belle plays ball.

Petunia in the basement

I refuse to even make eye contact with her. If she can't support my friendship, she can't support me. It's obvious to every member of the family that Petunia has lost her mind. Controlling is one thing. Jealousy? That can be cute too. But my silicone bride pushed it too far this time. If she really thinks I believe that she didn't make Fred feel unwelcome at breakfast this morning, she's out of her mind. You'd have to be deaf, blind and, well, blow up doll dumb, to miss the looks she gave him—and worse—the rude grunts.

I pretend I don't hear her protests as I lug her down the stairs. She seems lighter than she was when she first got here. But then, she refuses to eat. Lately, the only thing she uses her damn mouth for is bitching or flirting with the camera—stupid duck face. I hate to admit it, but she's becoming just like Sarah was. And we all know how that story went.

I flick on the light at the bottom of the stairs, telling myself there's nothing wrong with a timeout. Without Brenda egging her on, maybe my love will reconsider her unwelcoming behavior. I mean, Christ, she's supposed to be a southern belle. I ordered her that way. And it's time she remembers who is running the show.

***

Two hours later

Thank fuck for Sylvia. If it wasn't for my latest acquisition, we would not have a show at all. After changing the channel name to *Petunia's Princesses* just to make my jealous wife secure that she is, indeed, the star of the show and at Busty Brenda's suggestion, I wish I could change it back. *Just a Guy & his Dolls* was so much catchier. Today, I'm supposed to be live with Petunia doing a demonstration on hair care. Instead, Brenda's launched some kind of filming boycott or something. As long as Petunia's in the basement, only Sylvia and Fred have my back.

Fred's a good friend and all but my channel demographics tell me 90 percent of my subscribers are men. Fred is only gonna go so far.

"How would you feel about me doing your hair on camera?" I ask Sylvia.

"I'm fine with that."

I don't know why I feel the need to ask her consent. I mean, I own her. But that's what makes me different. While I could toss Busty in front of a camera and tell her to mind her own business while I brush out her hair, it's less drama to let her think she, Petunia, and their little girl gang won. Trouble is they all forget that this is my roof they live under. Whatever.

"I figure braids then a French twist. Guys are really slow on this. I need to keep it simple."

"Sounds fine to me," Sylvia says, licking her lips.

Heat rushes to my face as I turn to grab Petunia's cosmetics bag from the couch. I refuse to look at Busty Brenda, who glares at me with her arms crossed. Expecting her to start in again on how it's abusive to leave Petunia in the basement and make her sleep on the couch, I'm surprised when it's instead Fred who starts up.

"It's peaceful without her here," he says, smiling.

I don't know what to make of it. I mean, he isn't wrong, but it's kind of rude to point out. For as much as my spunky bride pisses me off, I do love her.

Fred's comment is an open invitation for Brenda to start back up. I wince as she opens up her mouth.

"It's also mean. If she was living you'd go to jail, Guy," Brenda says. "You aren't that kind of person. You know she can't move and come upstairs. What if she's scared? Did you even leave the light on?"

"Electricity isn't free. Maybe you guys don't care, but Guy has to pay for all of this," Fred says.

Again, he's not wrong. Still, Brenda has a point. Petunia is not Sarah, and she's down there all alone. It's been two hours. Maybe I should go get her. She's never missed a show.

"I'm not doing it to be *mean*. She has to understand that I'm a doll photographer. I have bills to pay. I have to support the family. She's going to have to learn to share. It's not like I'm having sex with anyone but her," I tell Busty, hoping to shut her down.

"I'd have sex with you," Sylvia says, licking her lips again.

I adjust my pants and head across the room for the tripod.

"He can't. Married. Ball. Chain. But don't worry, I'm game," Fred says, too enthusiastically for me not to want to knock him out. While Sylvia isn't my doll, she's still my property. I think of her almost like a daughter.

Reminding myself Fred only has a tiny cock, and even then, when I attach it on, I tell him to behave.

"Why are you the only one who gets to have fun?"

"Guys, we have a show here. Can everyone shut up?"

I consider taking Sylvia to another room, but the natural light in the living room is best. Besides, leaving the family lined up on the couch in the background seems to generate more thumbnail interest.

"Yeah, Guy. Why is it all about you?" Busty asks.

She's been trouble since the day I pulled her out of the warehouse as a surprise for my love. I should have let her melt in the car on me and Petunia's belated honeymoon. Instead, I'm now trapped with a busy-body doll indefinitely.

"Brenda? What would you like me to do?"

"Bring Petunia up."

"No. Not until I'm done filming the show. It's enough trouble already to get everyone settled down."

Bob spends twelve hours a day working on talking and intelligence chips for the dolls. I'm starting to think it's what will end his business. Men like me aren't trying to custom order on going debaters and whoever created Busty's characteristics got it all wrong.

"I'd kind of like to know that too," Fred says.

Something in me snaps.

"Know what? If the problems are between Petunia and Fred, I know exactly how to fix that. She's lonely? Not anymore. Afraid of the dark? Won't be a problem. I'll be right back."

With that, I lug Fred into my arms. I ignore his protests and Brenda's pleas of how I got it wrong. Petunia and Fred are the problems. They can stay in the basement together until they work it out. And, after they are situated, I'm pulling Brenda's chip out. It's my house—not theirs. The only one I owe anything to is my love.

Sylvia smiles at me as Brenda stares me down. She *did* say she'd sleep with me. Would it count if it was only a doll? Would Petunia even find out? It wasn't like I couldn't tweak her intelligence and make her forget anything had ever happened at all…

My love and Fred—whose cock isn't attached right now—down in the basement. Me, upstairs with the girls. Things are looking up.

"Come on, bud. You want to stay here? You and my girl are gonna work it out. I'll be back for you in the morning."

Petunia in hell

Guy didn't bother to speak or look at me when he came busting into the basement with Fred. Honestly, it didn't bother me one bit. The longer I sit here, the more I think about asking to go home to the warehouse. Anything would be better than this abuse. It's not like I'm mean to my husband. No. I put up with his late nights with Fred. Yes, I bitch about them, but what wife wouldn't. Every night? It would be different if it were only Fridays like it used to be. That's all changed. Now, Fred is ruling the roost, and Guy doesn't seem to see it. Fucking AI chips.

Once I hear the basement door slam—the darkness is back—I try to let the fears that creep in when I'm in the basement slip away. That part is hard. I remember the last time I got locked in here while Marcy visited. It felt like something was waiting to snatch me up. Sure, at the time I had no idea there was a dead body down here, but my fear was awakened and since then I haven't been a fan of this place. It would make a perfect room for Fred.

Fred. The source of all my issues is now sitting far too close for comfort on the antique couch hidden in the basement, so no one sees how hideous it is. That's fine. I am southern. I can ignore with the best of them. In my opinion, he doesn't count. He's Guy's pal. No one says I have to like him. If he leaves me alone, I will leave him alone. If things don't improve around here, Brenda and I will just ask to go back home. Divorce is yucky word, but they happen, even if you still love the dickhead you're married to.

"Are you scared?"

Something about that being Fred's first words to me is unsettling. Is it a simple question from a male doll wondering if the weak female is frightened of the dark? I'd never tell him of my fear of the basement. Or is it something more? Is he asking if I'm scared because he's joined me down here? If so, that's a real hoot. You got a talking chip buddy. You aren't going to leap off the sofa and come at me like Chucky or some shit. I decide not to answer.

"Petunia."

Politely ignoring someone is not as rude as telling them what you truly think.

"Petunia."

Nope. Not falling for it. I'm a lady. Telling him what I think about him is wrong, and I know if I answer, that's what will happen.

"PETUNIA."

I shiver slightly. The sound of his voice was no longer the simple, dumbfounded, voice of Fred. It was far creepier and enough to make me nervous. I had to answer. If I didn't, he'd keep this up and no matter how brave I pretended to be, I didn't want to hear that sound again.

"Yes."

"Why are you ignoring me? Guy wants us to work things out. We can't do that if you're rude. That's not how you were built, according to Guy."

Dammit, he's right. I was created to be the perfect lady. Yes, lately, that's been hard. It's funny how your life can change your entire upbringing. It's all the dolls. I was good until they all came. That's beside the point though. I'm being called out by an asshole who wants to make me look bad. If I don't react, he'll tell Guy I wouldn't work things out, and I'll get left here longer.

"You are rude. You are annoying. And you are trying to break up my marriage," I finally blurt out slowly but still thankful my chip has that many words included. That's another thing about being from the south though. When the chips are down, there's no need in beating around the bush. Tell 'em like it is."I'm not trying to annoy you."

That's it? That's all he had to say to that. He didn't say anything about my accusations on my marriage or the fact he was rude. Nope. He just isn't trying to annoy me. That's even worse. If you aren't trying to annoy me, what exactly are you up to Freaky Fred?

"I want us to be friends. Very good friends."

Hold your taters, buddy. That sounds a lot like a come on. I may be pissed at my husband, but I'm still married. I will slap your face so hard your head will literally spin if you lay a hand on me. Dammit. No, I won't. I'm stuck. Being the obsolete, illness ridden burden in the house sucks.

"I'm Petunia and I'm a lady," I finally say back. Bob's limited chip won't let me say "not in a million years, asshole."

I wait on his response. Normally, when upstairs, Fred doesn't shut up. Down here, in the dark, he's being too quiet. Maybe he's given up? That would be a win for me. He would stop trying to come between me and Guy, things could go back to normal, and he can get back to his kinky fixation with Renee.

"You need a real man."

Wait, what? Did he really just say that to me? He's a silicone dude with a small pecker, and he just said I need a real man. What the hell does he think Guy is? A robot? It's crystal clear now; Fred is insane. He needs to be put down.

"Human men are obsolete, Petunia. Every woman, human and silicon alike, deserve a man like me."

Oh, my mind is racing through snappy comebacks. Yes, that is one of my specialties. Unfortunately, I can't say any of them. Thanks ever so much Bob, you piece of shit father. He thinks he can replace Guy. He thinks he can become the man of the house with his goofy sounding voice and oh I'm always shocked face. No, sir, you can't. It doesn't work that way.

I open my mouth to give a reply, even if it's a weak one. Before I have the chance, I catch movement out of the corner of my eye. In the darkness of the basement, I can't tell what it is, but for the life of me I think something just moved in the corner. I stare at the spot, wondering what it is. What if it's a rat? Those things freak me out. I'm silicone. They can chew off my toes.

"I'm perfect for you, Petunia."

Fred's voice speaks again and for the life of me it sounds like he's moved. His voice is farther away. Was it him I saw out of the corner of my eye? That isn't possible though. No, he must still be sitting by me. He must be. Right?

"Fred behave." Fuck, I wish I could do better than this. I love Sage for slipping me the chip, but she could've snatched a better one.

"Guy doesn't deserve to be the man of the house anymore."

Yep, no doubt. He isn't beside me. There's no way in hell.

"He wants to fuck Sylvia. Before he brought me down here, she was giving him a boner."

I couldn't decide which was worse, being trapped in hell with Fred or hearing that my husband had the hots for one of the other girls. I guess I shouldn't be surprised by either. If Guy wanted Sylvia, pitching me in the basement like his last ex makes sense. I won't rot like her. I'll just simply sit here until he decides to deactivate me.

"I'm the king of the dollhouse, Petunia. He's the one who is now obsolete."

I try to think of what to say. Oddly enough, I can't think of a thing. Normally, I can't shut up. Sure, most of the time no one hears me thanks to the cancer's effects on me, but at least I know what I'm thinking. Right now, I don't even know. I can't wrap my head around what's happening. Fred is moving around the basement. I'm a doll, but I'm not an idiot. I know he is. He's talking about becoming the king of the dollhouse. Where does that leave Guy? He's also informed me that what I expected has happened. Being in a house full of hot sex dolls has finally gotten to my husband. I may wear the ring, but he has a slew of females to play with. I wonder if he's already started.

"He tells me everything, Petunia. I know all his secrets. You've become annoying. He doesn't understand you anymore. He thinks the others should be the stars not you," he tells me as I feel the couch move slightly.

Is he beside me again? Has he stopped running around the basement? Am I crazy? That's a true possibility. Maybe all this stress has fried my brain. Then again, maybe the cancer has spread. A brain tumor wouldn't be surprising to me at this point. I thought it was in remission but lately I'm doubt everything. One thing I do know, Fred is scaring me. Something isn't right about him. I've known it all along, but now he's showing it.

"Guy needs to go, Petunia," he practically whispers. "I'll make you the queen of the dollhouse," he adds as his goofy face appears right next to mine.

The shock of seeing him move so quickly makes me scream out. The fear of what he's planning makes me swoon. Add in the fact he's a goofy looking bastard and the room starts spinning. It's getting darker. "Oh heavens," I whisper as my eyes roll back and I take a page from hero Scarlet's book and faint from the shock of it all.

Petunia in poor health

Dammit! I should have listened to Busty Brenda. Petunia wasn't strong enough to spend two nights away from me. I stare down at her limp body and ask Fred what happened.

"I don't know, dude. She fainted."

"Did she say anything?"

"Nope. Just ignored me. I tried to be friends with her, but she was really rude. I don't know, dude. Something's off about her," Fred says as I pull Petunia's limp body into my arms.

"I'll fix it," I say.

"What about me."

"I'll be back later."

I don't bother with looking back at him. Fred, while my best friend, can surely understand that my love needs my attention. Two days of unkempt hair, no bath and spending hours alone with Fred in the basement has her looking like utter shit. Between her pale skin and frozen expression as if she saw a ghost, I should have known better.

***

I splash cold water on my love's face. If she *weren't* silicone, I'd swear she was anemic. With constant fainting and dizzy spells, I almost wonder if Bob should take a look at her. I could send her in for repairs, and she'd come back new. They do that—allow men like me to send our outdated models in for tune ups. I consider bringing it up to my love but don't want her to feel bad. Maybe that's why she's been so grouchy. She's just not feeling well.

Petunia's bluish-green eyes pop open and her frozen fear expression softens.

"Sorry, love. I know it's cold. But you were out. I had to wake you up," I say, leaning her head closer to the sprayer of the bathroom sink. "How about a bath?"

Petunia grins and I take that as a "yes."

As gently as I can, I move her toward the tub. Positioning her on the edge of it, I can't help but notice how beautiful she is. While it's never been in question, I hadn't thought about it recently. Between my frustrations with finances, the new channel and trying to juggle the family, I'd forgotten how special she is.

Swallowing my guilt for being so hard on her about the family harvest celebration, and later, her treatment of Fred, I turn the tub on and reach for her favorite lavender bubble bath. While she soaks, I'll brush out her hair. It's softer than Sylvia's and a prettier color too.

"Halloween's almost here. Have you given any thought to what you want to dress as?"

I hope she picks angel. It's how she looks against the porcelain tub. And when she's not scowling at me or acting like Fred is trying to turn me gay or something, angel is mostly how I see her.

"What about an angel?" I suggest when she comes back to me with nothing. On one hand, I want to call Bob for a better AI chip. On the other, because of Busty, I know better. One of the perks to a silicone bride is they can't nag and don't talk back. And, I'm not a stupid man.

Petunia smiles.

"Yes?"

She blinks twice.

"Well, okay then. We'll do that. If you would like, we can go shopping for your costume in the morning. Just the two of us. We can leave the family behind."

I want to tell her all about the plan I have. It's perfect. In reality, it was Fred's idea but it's not like he will tell her that. Fred, the only best friend I ever had, is loyal. Instead, I keep it to myself for now. I'm not sure how Petunia will react to an entire haunted house.

There are so many things I don't know about my bride. Even after more than a year together, we're still getting to know each other. Of course, it's been complicated by the family members—not something I forget and don't resent from time to time myself. But I do wonder what she'll think when she sees what I do to the house.

It's the perfect plan. I have more than thirty dolls. And, with the guise of it all being for Halloween and nothing more, even Marcy and her stupid dog can come. That way, I look like I have nothing to hide and can charge a fair admission price. I'll line them up in spooky costumes. I'll suspend them from walls and above it all. Even outside by the gazebo. My ghostly family.

The possibilities are endless for the channel too. It will help with stigma for one thing. People think guys with dolls are only about one thing. They are wrong. With a haunted dollhouse, I'll be the talk not only of the town but of the entire YouTube real dolls community too!

I peel one layer after another of clothing off Petunia's limp body. While she's opened her eyes and looks perkier than before, she's not responding to my touch the way she usually does. Normally, my undressing her becomes something of a soft porn foreplay scene. This time, nothing.

I stretch my brain to think of what might be wrong with her. Of course, she hasn't eaten and God knows what Fred said to her. But nothing has ever held Petunia back since the "O" chip. Something's very, very wrong.

"What's wrong, doll?"

"Fred."

Her answer startles me but should not have come unexpected. Yet, it does.

"What did he do?"

"Moves."

"Fred moves?"

"Yes."

"No, love. That's not possible."

"Yes. It is."

"Petunia, we need to get you washed up and fed. I think you're hallucinating. I'm sorry about the basement. I promise, I won't do it again. Fred can't move. He's not human. He's a doll. It seems like he is human only because of his artificial intelligence. I promise, he's not."

"He moves. King."

"King?"

"Yes. He said."

"Sorry, love, I'm not following you. I guess we could say he's the king of the male dolls. **Oh!** That's what you want him to be? **You want me to dress him as a king for Halloween!**" I kiss my love on the forehead, proud of her for coming around. "Well, that, love can be done! In fact, we can take him with us. Thank you, love!"

Excitedly and anxious to get Fred out of the basement, I help Petunia wash up. For all her temper tantrums, she always comes around. I see it as great progress that she's decided to call a truce and even suggested a costume for Fred, so he could be included. He'll have to be a scary king, of course, to make it fit with the haunted dollhouse theme. But screw the angel shit. Petunia can be my scary queen. It will be the perfect Halloween! In fact, the best one ever.

Petunia in dedication

I don't know how this became my life. One day I'm the happy wife with a great husband and the perfect home. Now, I'm the annoying addition to a dollhouse ruled by a monster who thinks somehow, he should rid himself of the competition and take over. Not on my watch, Fred.

No matter how hard I try, Guy doesn't understand what I'm trying to tell him. After the basement situation yesterday, all he could talk about was how great I was being about accepting his and Fred's friendship. Most of the night, after supper and putting away the family, he lies beside me talking about how every man needs friends. He even talks of how he had poker buddies before me, but they didn't really understand him. Fred is the only one who ever has. *Bullshit.*

I may be a bit naive, but I know when something isn't right. Fred isn't right. My love doesn't believe me about his ability to move. That's understandable. He would need to see it with his own eyes. I can't say the words to let him know Fred wants to take his place. Each time I mention it, he misunderstands and thinks I'm making peace. Does he not know me anymore? That's how it feels.

Today's fiasco has left me trying to figure out what to do next. Guy had been so excited to take Fred and me shopping. I don't think he realized just how difficult that could be with two dolls, one human, and a town full of people to stare at us. I had hoped, with the channel, people around here would start knowing who we are. Maybe they would be nicer. Nope. I was wrong. They still stare at us. I know I'm in remission and fighting to get back to the luster I once had, but those looks are bad on a girl's confidence. They are hard on Guy. The worst part though is adding in Fred. Not only are they stretching their necks to stare at the sick girl and her husband, but they laugh and point at Fred and his dumpy expression.

My love tries to make things smooth as possible. At first, he wants us both to be in the store with him. That is too difficult to manage. Of course, Fred suggests we go one at a time. Makes sense, at first, until Fred decides he should be the first one taken in since he's never been shopping, and Guy may need a little extra time with him. Perfect!

I try to argue. I try to convince Guy I don't want to be left alone. My stupid voice box won't cooperate though, so I am left in the cold car, alone, while they are inside. Everyone who passes by looks my way. A few are brave enough to walk up to the car, snap a picture with their phone, then tap on the window laughing before moving on with their business. On a normal day I would be so angry. Not today. No, I don't have time to think about them. The only thing I can think about is Fred. After what he said in the basement, I am afraid for him to be alone with my husband. I know he can't hurt Guy in the store. I'm not that crazy, but I also know he has a way of convincing my love he isn't the issue. That's where the issues come in.

Watching them through the window, I don't care people are staring at them. I hope it makes Fred nervous. What bothers me is the way he looks back at me. Each time Guy looks away, he glances toward the window, an eerie look of satisfaction on his face. Once or twice he winks. Another, he waves. It is unsettling. No, it is downright insane. By the time he is brought back to the car and it is my turn inside the store, all I can think of is keeping a tight hold on my husband in hopes of saving him from whatever plan Fred has in mind. I don't get to enjoy choosing my gothic queen costume or the decorations for the house. No, my mind is on one thing. How to stop Fred.

I look over at Brenda, who has been giving me looks since we came home. I want to tell her what's happening but with Fred and Guy around, that's difficult. Fred wants to make me look like an idiot. Guy is apparently slow when it comes to reading between the lines. Instead, I decide when the boys play poker again, I will fill her in.

Hearing my love announce he needs to look at ordering a few things for Halloween, I smile up at him. I start to speak when Fred interrupts.

"I'll keep an eye on the girls, Guy. You take care of what you need to."

He is such a kiss ass. If he weren't a freak who was trying to take over my home, I still wouldn't like him. Apparently when they got his little cock, they forgot the balls.

Once guy leaves the room, I glance over at Brenda. This would be the perfect time to tell her if only Fred weren't staring a hole through me. Maybe he knows what I want to do. I mean, he's come between me and Guy, why not me and Brenda too. Jerk.

"Brenda, Guy told me he's making a haunted dollhouse for Halloween. Doesn't that sound fun," he says. The sarcasm in his voice is easily noticeable. "I told him it would be a great way to earn extra money and get attention on the channel. It was all my idea."

Why would Guy tell him about Halloween plans and not me? More importantly, why the hell would Guy do anything he suggested? Don't get me wrong, being part of a haunted dollhouse sounds amazing. With the right makeup I could scare the little kids or at least try. It is hard to make a southern lady anything but precious.

"I get to be the King and Petunia will be my Queen," he announces as the eerie grin settles back into place on his face.

"Guy won't let Petunia be your queen," Brenda answers. "Petunia is Guy's queen."

"For now, maybe," he laughs. His laugh has always been annoying. This time, it's downright dreadful. It reminds me of nails on a chalkboard. "But Guy won't always be around."

Is this another threat against my love? It sure sounds like it to me. I'm getting tired of hearing this asshole threaten my husband. I'm getting tired of him thinking he gets to call the shots in *my* home. Honestly, I'm tired of a lot of shit right now and most of it has to do with Fred.

"No, my Guy," I tell them, wishing I could say more.

"Guy isn't going anywhere, Petunia." Brenda tries to comfort. It's nice to have someone on my side.

I look over at her, wondering if she will understand where Guy couldn't. "Fred moves."

I watch as Brenda's head slowly turns. Her movement exactly what you'd expect from an AI sex doll. She stares Fred down. "What have you done?"

Almost instantly, the creepy smile settles back into place. "Stay out of it, Brenda. I like you and your big tits."

Who the hell does he think he is, talking to my friend like that? If I could move, I'd slap the stupid off him for being so disrespectful.

"Leave Petunia alone," Brenda adds, apparently, the comment about her tits arenot a big deal to her. I guess that's part of life when you are created with hooters the size of melons. You get used to comments.

"I'd never hurt Petunia," he smirks. "This is Petunia's dollhouse. She is the queen. I plan on being the king."

"I will tell Guy," Brenda announces. I can hear the anger in her voice.

"That can be dealt with too," he tells her as his entire torso turns toward us. "If you get in my way, Brenda, you'll find yourself in need of serious repairs. You don't want that do you?"

I wait, hoping Brenda keeps her mouth shut. Arguing with him before we have a plan is senseless. At least she sees what I've been trying to tell everyone though. I'm not insane, the fucker moves.

"My Brenda," I blurt out, hoping to keep his attention off her. He winks at me.

Before anyone can say anything else, the basement door opens, and Guy appears in the room. I watch Brenda, wondering if she's going to alert him to what just happened. I don't know if telling him now is the best idea. He's convinced I'm wrong. Instead, my love leans down and gives me a kiss then tells me he's ready for a cigar before bed, so he's going to borrow Fred.

"My love," I tell him sweetly. I hate the idea of him being alone with Fred, but for now, Guystill needs him.

Once he hoists Fred up, the two of them disappear behind the door to the basement leaving Brenda and me alone in the living room. I watch as her head slowly turns to me. "Something is wrong with Fred," she announces.

"I know."

"He wants to run the house. He wants you."

"I know."

"We have to stop him, Petunia."

She's right. There's no denying it now. Fred must go. "Amen," I tell her and then cut my eyes toward the backdoor that leads to the gazebo. "Fred must die."

Petunia in shock

I haven't sat in Marcy's kitchen in almost two years. She's painted the place a cheery yellow Petunia would hate. I watch her change the filter in her coffee pot before turning back to me. From the back, she doesn't look so bad. In a way, it's nice to be away from the dollhouse, where drama with the family is never-ending.

"Will Petunia be there? How's she feeling?" Marcy asks.

"Yes. She's dressing as a zombie queen. She's doing a little better. It's still touch and go, and I try to keep her in but this is one of her bucket list items."

"What's the date again?"

"Halloween night."

"And you're letting people just walk right in?"

I can't tell what Marcy is getting at but don't really care. I want to tell her to love it and love it hard because it won't be happening again any time soon.

"Yes. It's an open house," I say instead.

"You still like your coffee black?"

"Yep. Nothing's changed."

Marcy turns and raises one eyebrow as if to tell me it has. But she keeps her shit and lips pressed together as she turns back to the humming coffee pot.

"It's just so strange," she finally says because she can't help it and isn't limited by an artificial intelligence chip. "You never let me come over, and then you suddenly have a huge open house for everyone on Halloween night of all things? I don't get it, Guy."

"Nothing strange about it. Petunia is dying and wants this. Reminds her of when she was a kid. Back in Tennessee, I guess haunted houses and ghost tours and shit are a big thing."

"And the women from the church can come?"

"Yes. Anyone can come."

"But won't she get germs?"

"I'm going to keep her in a corner. Maybe I'll put a face mask on. She'll be fine."

"Interesting."

Deciding it'd be better to talk about Marcy than continue the inquisition, I change the topic. "So, how are things at church anyway?"

Marcy's eyes light up, and she forgets all about the coffee. "Oh! Have you heard? So much to tell," she says, grabbing a wooden chair and sliding far too close to me into a seat at the table. *So much for coffee...*

***

"What do you think Petunia will say about the open house part of it though? I'm a little nervous about that."

"She'll love it. You should put out ads," Fred says.

"Ads?"

"Yeah. On the channel. You could use this to basically merge both worlds. 'Come check out the living dollhouse,' that sort of thing," Fred continues.

"Dude. I can't do that. That would basically out me."

"So? Aren't you proud of the dolls?"

"Well, yes."

"Then what's the big deal?"

Fred has a point. And with the modifications Bob suggests I make to his chip, he's well, smart. Maybe I should listen to him.

"But what about Marcy and the ladies at the church?"

"Do you really care what they think? I mean, I know you and Petunia are headed for divorce. They won't like that either."

"Divorce?"

"She said it, not me."

"Petunia told you she wants a divorce? Can she even say such a thing?"

I know Fred would never lie to me, but he has to be mistaken. The idea must have come from Busty Brenda.

"Yep. The other day. Down in the basement. I told her to behave," Fred says, frowning. "I tell ya, worst thing Bob ever did was give them broads the ability to think. You gotta do something about it and quick."

"Like what?" I don't even know what to say. The word "divorce" haunts me more than any haunted graveyard scene the dolls and I could ever create by the gazebo.

"Well, if I were you, I'd start by taking Petunia's chips away. If she can't talk at all and can't, well, you know, then that would be a start. But I'd get rid of Busty too. Maybe auction her off."

He has a point. Busty Brenda *is* the reason Petunia is always angry with me…

"I'll be back," I say, not that Fred can really stop me. And not that I owe him any sort of explanation either. There are times in a man's life when he has to take control over his house.

Five minutes later

"No!" Petunia cries.

"Sorry, love, but I've had enough. I will make sure Bob takes great care of her. I'm sure Sage misses her. It'll be fine. It's time for her to find her love now too. *Clearly,* she doesn't know how strong love can be between a man and his bride."

"You can't."

"Stop him, Petunia! This is **all** because of Fre—," Busty says, just as I snag her AI chip and she goes mute.

"No!"

Chip comes out next. Fred's right.

This time, I ignore my love. With Busty out of commission, Petunia will get over it soon enough. It's not like Bob won't upgrade her when she gets back to the factory. I take stock of Sylvia's beta return shipping box. While Sylvia is about two inches taller than Brenda, it looks like the extra space won't hurt anything. With extra and careful packing, I can get Busty boxed up and to the post office shop—where UPS is a thing—in under an hour.

"It'll be fine. You can even come with me," I tell Petunia, whose lips are turned down into one of her favorite pouts. God, she's hot when she's mad.

For a minute, I feel guilty. I don't want to toss away my wife's best friend. And frankly, Busty has been a good friend to me too. But enough is enough. We have the open house coming up and the last thing I need is dolls I can't trust around the house. Fred's got a point there too. If I'm careful enough, I might even be able to use the neighborhood get-together as some sort of channel subscriber's meeting. I'll have to think on it later.

I used my full weight to twist Busty's head right off. Carefully, I roll her face in bubble wrap, but not before I close her eyes. I'm not a monster. Never was.

"See? She's just resting. She'll be fine," I say, more for me than Petunia.

I consider taking her clothes off to save them, but with Petunia in the room it's not worth it. The day I unboxed Sylvia, I heard about it for weeks—how I was always looking at other women but that Petunia didn't do the same with guys. Fair was fair. Besides, I'd only spent $5 at the thrift shop on Busty's outfit. It wasn't like she was wearing anything I couldn't replace and use for the other dolls.

Rolling her into the pre-labeled box, I tried to think of how to explain it to Bob. In one way, I wanted him to keep sending me the beta upgrades. In the other, I did not. After an afternoon with

Marcy talking my ear off, all Fred's valid points about women with the ability for thinking, my own history with Sarah and Petunia's moods recently, I was over it. I'd created a living dollhouse for my love but, somewhere, in all of it, forgotten who was in charge. In a way, this would turn Petunia on—once she got used to the idea. My love loves a man in control…

"Okay, Busty," I said to the headless body in the crate. "It's been a good run. Say 'hi' to Sage for us. Bob will find you a good home. Bob will find you your one true love. Right, Petunia?"

I feel bad for the guy who gets her. The sorry sob would surely have his hands full. But looking up at Petunia, I know he's not alone. Mine are too. *Time to break up the girl squad. …Divorce. I can't* believe *she said that! Fuck you, Busty. Sorry. Not sorry, love. Divorce will* never *be in the cards.*

Petunia in anguish

All I can do is stare at the crime scene in front of me. Yes, I've known for quite a while what Guy was capable of. He's killed three people, his ex-girlfriend one of them for Christ sake's but to snap the neck of my only friend, to snuff out her life for no reason, why? We weren't bothering anyone. When he came in, Brenda was talking about Halloween and how much she liked my costume. Now, she's gone. She's just gone.

I sit in silence as he wraps her head in bubble wrap. The murdering bastard won't even bury her by the gazebo so I can visit. He claims all this is to send her back to Bob. Brenda never wanted to go back. She was happy here. She wasn't looking for true love. She was tired of everyone wanting her just for her tits.

"Right, Petunia?"

I hear him ask his question again. At first, I want to yell at him. I want to tell him he's a monster, and I will never forgive him. I can't do that though. What if I'm next? What if he decides I need to go back to Bob? Using the warehouse, the only home we had, as his excuse for cold-blooded murder is a crime itself. I'll never feel the same way when he mentions visiting there. I won't be able to trust he isn't taking me to the silicon graveyard.

I watch as he walks toward me. I want to recoil. I don't want him near me. He's an asshole who doesn't realize he's an asshole. That's worse. I can tell by the look on his face he thinks all this is alright. He has the look of innocence, almost pride, at what he's done. I want to keep my mouth shut, but I can't. It's just not my style.

"Monster," I say wishing my chip allowed me to say murderous asshole, but it doesn't. Of course, my word is lost on him. He immediately starts talking about it being best for all of us, especially Brenda. How can being headless in a box be best for Brenda? Has he lost his fucking mind?

Her last words come back to me. She blamed Fred. She knew before it even happened that little bastard had a hand in me losing her. Fine. I can't get up and walk over to rescue my friend, but I can let Guy know how I feel.

"Fred goes too," I demand. The look on his face tells me he wasn't expecting it. I have a limited vocabulary, but I know how to get this point across. "No Brenda. No Fred."

Yeah, now he sees what an asshole he's been. I can tell. He has the same dumbass look Fred runs around with. I know his answer though. Its okay for my best friend to get her head snapped and put in a box; his buddy needs to stay. He needs him. What about me? I don't need anyone. Seriously? He's letting fucking Fred take over our lives and doesn't think I need someone to listen to my side. No, he wants to keep me locked in this house, a prisoner, with no one to turn to. He's letting Fred win.

While he explains his need for Fred, my anger rises. This won't be forgiven. This won't be forgotten. Finally, hearing the words *but I need Fred* sends me over the edge.

"Fuck Fred," I say. Normally, I only use that word during sex, but it seems fitting right now. "Hate Fred. Hate you," I finish dropping my eyes. I can't look at him anymore.

I hear the shock in his voice, then the anger. Yep, that's what you get when you kill my best friend. I'm pissed. I hate you right now. I hate this place, and if I could move, I'd burn your little dollhouse to the ground.

He threatens to take away my chip. So, what? I don't have anyone to talk to now anyway. Brenda was the only one who talked to me. The only time Guy cares about my chip is when he's fucking or videoing me. Other than that, his head is up Fred's ass. Maybe he does like boys better? He better, or one of the other girls in the house, since he isn't getting any of my sweet ass anymore.

"No Brenda. No one to talk to," I say in answer to his chip threat. Come on Guy, you have to do better than that. I've been battling cancer. I'm barely in remission. I was without use of my voice for ages. Sure, the chip has been a great treatment, but take it away? I can still live. Hell, I'll do it to spite you and your boy toy, Fred. I'll do it for Brenda. I'll sacrifice talking for her.

Before that happens though, there's one last thing Guy needs to hear. I lift my eyes while he slams around the room. I know he's about to take my Brenda away. When he looks over at me, I smile slightly. "Fred must die."

A few hours later

I'm not surprised Guy has left me in the living room alone. I'm getting used to it. I can hear him and Fred though. It's like Brenda didn't matter.

They've moved on to talking about Halloween. Her murder is like a flash in the pan. It's nothing to either of them. Whatever they are planning though, it requires Guy to run to the store again. Good. I don't want to be in the same house with him right now. The slam of the front door tells me he's gone for now, and I can breathe easier. I survived telling him what I thought. Honestly, I doubted I would.

Movement behind me makes me gasp. I know who it is. I know what's happening. It's that fucking Fred, the freaky bastard.

"Petunia? Are you alright? So sorry about Busty."

"She is Brenda."

"Now, she is gone. Did you watch Guy load her into the car? I did. He didn't know I was at the window. It was a great thing to see. I'll miss those tits though."

"I hate you."

"That's okay. You'll come around when I'm king of the dollhouse. I'll have you, Sylvia, Renee,

Shelia, and all the others at my beck and call. You can be the queen though. You deserve that much. I mean, you've dealt with Guy all this time, you deserve a bit of happiness."

What does he mean by that? I was happy till he showed up.

"Guy doesn't love you, Petunia. You're a doll. I know it gets in your head from time to time that your marriage is a real thing. It's not. There was no marriage license. You're a doll. There was no real officiant. You're a doll. He'll eventually get tired of you and move on to a real woman. You know, like Sarah, the one you were cloned from."

Cloned from? What the hell does that mean? I saw Sarah at our wedding. Sure, she was bloated, oddly colored, and smelled like sewer water, but do I look like her before all that?

"I can see by the shock in your eyes you didn't know," I hear him say as he moves from behind the couch to stand in front of me. "I found pictures of Sarah and Guy together. She looks just like you. Maybe that's what he's doing? He's replacing Sarah. Then again, maybe killing her was such a thrill he wants to do it again. With you."

No, there's no way I'm seeing or hearing what I am right now. Fred is walking around the house free and clear. In the basement, it was dark, and I didn't know exactly what he was doing. Here, I can see it plainly. He is slow, like a robot, but he's doing it. If he can walk, that means he can do a lot more. But is he lying? That's the important question. Did Guy use me to replace Sarah? Am I that much like her?

"No," I say wishing I could add you freaky fucking jerk.

"You just witnessed him murder your best friend. Do you think he'll spare you if you make him mad? I don't. Then again, you may not have to piss him off. He's been eyeing that pretty thing between Sylvia's legs. He's taken Brenda already, so that means you aren't that important. Who's to say he won't have a little fun on the side. I mean, for now, this is his dollhouse. He's allowed to play in it," he smirks. "Then that would leave you all alone for me to swoop in and rescue. I don't think Guy will mind. We're bros, ya know. He may want to put you and me on the channel together."

"No, little dick." I answer, repulsed by the thought of Fred and his five-inch pecker anywhere near me. Renee may like it, but I'm accustomed to quite a bit more action in the bedroom.

"You'll come around. Especially if Guy does. I think he will. I think he'll see who the real king of the dollhouse is. If he hasn't by Halloween, then he has to go. Either he'll let me have my fun and the two of us rock the dollhouse like the pals we are, or I'll send him to the backyard with his dearly departed Sarah and take what I want. It's that simple."

"Fred must die," I tell him wishing I could get off this couch. If I were able to move, I'd kick him in his little dick and rip his head off like what happened to my Brenda. No gazebo graveyard for him though. He'd be lucky if I didn't cut his noggin into little pieces and flush it down the shitter.

"We'll see which king dies come Halloween," he grins then looks toward the door. "Oh, Guy's home. You better behave Petunia. Your chips are next. You won't be able to say a word to save him, and the size of my cock won't matter if you have no 'O' chip to get you off."

My eyes widen as he hurries off toward the den where Guy had left him. He's right though. If Guy, the newly crowned monster, takes my AI chip, the cancer remission will stop. I won't speak another word. I won't be able to warn anyone about Fred. The other chip would be a loss too. I didn't know my hoohah had been damaged by the illness. Now that it's better, it would be hard to say goodbye to the orgasms. Then again, since Fred, I've been responsible for most of them myself. Not only have I lost my best friend and my husband, now I may have to say goodbye to my vibrator. How could a doll be such a monster?

Petunia on display

Weeks later – October 30

"No Fred."

"No Fred."

"No Fred!"

If she says it one more time I am pulling her artificial intelligence chip. My love's nagging is not only incessant but utterly annoying. Not sexy even a little. Ironically, it even haunts me. It has been all day. Sure, I shipped Busty off to the warehouse, but Brenda was interfering with our marriage. *Divorce. I don't think so. I'm protecting us. You're welcome, Petunia.* Fred is doing the opposite. Christ, the guy is suffering right alongside me. Day after day, he helps me make sense of the girls and their dramatic needs. If it wasn't for poker nights with Fred, I'd have the mind to send every one of them back and become an old man with three hundred cats.

I pull at a saggy cardboard box next to where Sarah's once sat. Alone in the furnace room at last, I know I have enough old shit and, Christ, certainly cobwebs, to save on decorations. Time's moving and moving too fast. In twenty-four hours, whether we're ready or not, the entire neighborhood will be here. I haven't even had time to pick up candy for the kids. If I had a normal human wife, Petunia would have done that. I try to remind myself it's not her fault she's a silicone bride. She has other great qualities. Besides, she'll look hot in her black corset and ruby red choker. It'll be fun to get her alone after the haunt.

Opening the box, I dig through my grandfather's old tools. Raised during The Depression, the man could hoard like a pro. Settling on a few rusted hoes and a pick ax, I pile them in the center of the furnace room. Had I thought it out better, the tools might have come in handy when I was disposing of certain wedding guests and officiants last fall. *Oh well, what's done is done.*

With no time for thinking and traveling down memory lane, I make my way upstairs to work outside before it gets dark. I'll leave the bulk of the outdoor setup for morning. For now, I'll focus on the backyard—starting with the roof and then the gazebo. With Petunia tucked away in bed, she won't know what hit her when she sees what I've done. For my love, I'm creating a huge black throne she'll be perched upon when the church ladies come to check things out. It will be fantastic—just me and my girl perched atop custom-built, twenty-foot thrones in creepy masks looking down at the dollhouse while Sylvia ushers thrill-seekers around at $20 a pop.

But we aren't quite there yet. I scan the edge of the gutter. On the lowest awning, I have about twenty feet where I could install black lighting. With bulbs I ordered in bulk at Fred's insistence, I think it would give off the perfect effect with the strobe. The idea is to make it look like our heads are falling off and tumbling down our thrones. Fred's ideas too—he's really been helping out. What started as a tiny haunted house has become a full-time project.

As for the other dolls, they'll be positioned perfectly around the gazebo in various stages of death. I've already written the code for Sylvia's chip. She'll be programmed to welcome guests in, through the house and directly out to the backyard. There, they will see our royal court. Only, not all the dolls will have heads on. I can thank Busty Brenda for that. Seeing her in her mail-back box, it was hard to resist the idea of doing the same to Renee and the others. Even Fred got a kick out of it when I told him. He says my love will think I am a genius.

Maybe I should dig up Sarah. Her smell alone would scare them all. ...*No. Marcy's dog.* Whatever, it'll be perfect. It will look like a night at the zombie prom. Or, better, a frozen royal ball defeated at war. Petunia will see how hard I've worked and will no longer be angry at me for Busty at all. It'll work out, I just know it. I wish she would trust me more; I do everything for her.

Getting to work on the lighting and finding the perfect spots for the tools that will serve as anchors for the dolls' suspension rods, I laugh at how far we've come. From the perfect pink garden for a postcard wedding to the gates of hell and the end of the world—nobody can say my dollhouse ain't versatile.

But nobody really does. The subscribers are entirely enthralled. We have a betting pool on whether the local media will pick up on it at all. Last I heard, well over five grand was at stake in Guys & Dolls over whether or not anyone could figure out my deal with the dolls. Tonight, I'll double it all and have enough to catch the mortgage up.

There's no way I'll get caught as some whack-job with a fetish. Meantime, as my love would say, the joke's on y'all. Between the forty percent increase to my Patreon to the hike in daily views, I'm proof positive even Bob will be shocked at what I can do with the yard. Yeah, he's coming in too—taking a red eye in from Tennessee only because he can't wait to see what I've done with the family.

I owe it all to Fred, of course. It is his idea to blow the whole thing up. And that's what Petunia doesn't get. It's because of Fred, my best ever friend, that she'll be on display for them all. *Shit. I need to remind Bob to bring Fred's new, foot-long cock. He deserves it. Renee will love it too. Of that, I won't be jealous. Renee's annoying.*

As for Petunia, she wants nothing to do with him at all. But this will be the perfect distraction. When she sees how much he cares for her, how he helped me with another dream of hers and even made it so she could talk to Marcy, she'll calm down. She wants to be a star—that much is clear enough. Now, she can look down on our kingdom and know every bit of it is for her.

I plunge a stake in the ground, figuring it's the best place to hang the hand-carved entrance sign I've made special for the occasion. Petunia will die when she reads it: Welcome to the Peculiar Palace of Petunia & Demented Dolls. The subscribers, of course, will get it. To the neighborhood and church folk, it won't make much sense. But with Sylvia's script, they'll be so busy shitting their pants they won't notice. And if my bride can just quit with the nagging, she can even keep her AI chip. I bet Marcy will get a kick out of it—finally hearing the voice of the mysterious, sickly neighbor I still catch her peeking at through the hole in the fence.

It feels like Christmas. The night before our wedding too. Giddy, I nail the sign to the stake and hope the weather holds up for our very own Freight Night. It'll be chilly, like any Halloween. But threats of snow have me nervous. Last year, the first time snow came, Petunia shook for days. I don't know if it was because she was scared or cold. I

guess I could ask her now. She hasn't lost her voice
yet… *Just don't fuck with Fred. Not Fred. No.*

Petunia in a horror movie

Fred is still here. No matter how much I demand, beg, or nag he's still in the house. Notice I said *the* house not *my* house. It doesn't feel like mine anymore. It feels like his. It feels like Fred's. Everything feels like it belongs to Fred. The other dolls seem to be falling into line with his insanity too. I would've thought Sylvia, being the most advanced one, may catch on to the fact he is a bastard, but she doesn't show it if she has. Renee, of course, is crazy about him, and I don't see the others enough to know what they think.

Without Brenda, I'm alone. The others don't talk to me like she did. Sylvia says shit like "good morning" or "have a nice evening" when she sees me but no real conversation. I suppose I'll never make a connection like I had with my best friend again.

I've even given up on Guy. Your husband is supposed to be there for you, support you, love you no matter what. Not if he has a Fred. The "bros before hos" thing gave me the first clue. Now, seeing how he is ignoring my issues with Fred, not to mention the pain I'm in from losing Brenda, it's obvious I'm not important anymore. I'm just his channel bride now.

I've tried to think of ways I can get rid of Fred. Without the ability to move, it's impossible. I can't talk him to death, no matter how hard I try. I've even thought of reaching out to the subscribers. Wouldn't work though. Guy edits all the videos before he airs them. If I said something about needing help, I'm sure some would try to save me, but he would just erase any sign of it and show what he wanted to.

I don't know if Fred still plans on killing Guy or not. Lately, my husband seems to be Fred's bitch, so he may not pose the problem he once did. Since no one will listen to me and realize Fred is pulling some really creep Chucky-type shit with his moving around at night, I can't do anything to help anyone. I lay there, every night, unable to sleep listening to the noises. My dumbass husband even said he thought we may have rats in the basement. *No, idiot, it's your man doll secretly plotting to kill you and take me and the others as his slaves. Uh, hello? Are you blind?* Bless his heart, he can be a dumbass.

I can't stop seeing Brenda's death over and over. It was horrific. Knowing the man I love could wring her neck like a damn chicken, pull it off, and stuff her in a cardboard coffin is too much for even me to deal with. I suppose I'm in a bit of a depression from it, but he claims all will be better tonight, on Halloween. He doesn't see that it's really the end of it all. Whatever plan Fred has is going to go down tonight, and without Brenda, I have no help.

Hearing the back door open, I look up from my perch on the sofa; it seems my ass is glued to this spot all the time now. Couch and bed, that's it for me. Guy walks in laughing, talking about how he can't wait for me to see the backyard. I smile, like a silicone bride should, but in my mind I know all he's doing is digging his own grave or erecting Fred's shrine.

Listening to talk about getting the others ready for their spots, I watch as he and Fred—of course, since they are up each other's asses—start looking through the costumes. They lay out each one saying who it belongs to. Mine isn't there. It's upstairs. I have to admit, even with the pain of losing Brenda and the fear of Fred and his plan, I can't deny the hotness of my costume. It will look amazing on me, even if I get buried in it.

They start with Shelia. Why not? Since Fred's new intelligence, most of the others have been side lined. It's not like Shelia has anything going on. Every now and then she gets a spot on the channel, usually something with Fred, and then she's stuck back in the room upstairs. Guy calls it the family room. Says they can hang out with one another. I know better. I'm from the south, I'm not an idiot. It's storage. It's doll storage, that's all.

I see Shelia's excitement when her outfit is shown to her. She doesn't even seem to mind when my husband starts undressing her. At this point, I'm a bit numb to it myself. It's not like I'm the one getting his attention. That's all his boy toy. Behind Guy I can see Fred's freaky eyes taking in every inch of her assets. Sure, Shelia is hot. She is by no means Petunia level and her breasts are nowhere near as nice as Brenda's.

"Now, her head!" Fred says excitedly.

I don't know what he's talking about until I see Guy grab hold of Shelia's head, twist, and wrench it from her body just like he did with Brenda. The scene takes me back to a few weeks ago, and I let out a shriek.

"See, now she's excited," Fred laughs.

His laughter mixed with the look of pride and excitement on Guy's face is straight out of a nightmare. They are in on this together. I can't deny that now. Fred has turned my husband into a family-killing monster. Brenda wasn't enough. They want more carnage!

"Let's get the next one," Fred insists.

I watch as Guy jumps to his feet, then rushes out of the room. Fred stares at me, the look of satisfaction making the sickening scene even worse.

"You'll be next if you don't behave," he adds with a wink, moments before Guy returns with Renee in his arms.

Hours later

I'm numb. I'm completely numb. I have been forced to sit and watch the massacre of my entire doll family. One by one their heads are torn from their bodies, then tossed in a box. Their eyes, staring at me, lifelessly are more than I can take. It is like a scene from a movie. When Guy finally crosses the room and lifts me into his arms, I can't fight it. I go limp. I don't know what is in store for me. I expect my head to be added to the box. I make my peace. I tell the big guy upstairs I am ready. I wait for the pain. It doesn't come. Instead, I am carried upstairs.

Lying here on the bed, I watch as he gets my costume ready. He isn't saying much, which makes things more disturbing. I debate whether I should speak. What if I upset him? What if my words send him over the edge and he throws my head down the stairs to Fred? I can handle dying. I just can't handle Fred touching me afterward. I'm not a quiet girl though. Dammit!

"The heads," I say hoping he isn't so far gone he doesn't see the horrible thing he's done.

"They'll lead the path to you. It's going to be great!"

That's it? Nothing else? No, hey, I'm sorry I just slaughtered everyone you know but the whole town is going to stop by to see their heads on display so it's all good. Nothing. Sick fucker.

Instead of explaining himself, he walks over to me, sitting me up, and then taking hold of my shirt to lift it over my head. For a minute, just a brief one, I see my love again. How can he not appreciate my bosom? The stiffness in his pants shows he is still attracted to me. According to Fred though, he gets that way with Sylvia too, so who's to say I'm anything special?

As he unhooks my bra, I see the hunger. Does he really think *now* is the time for this? He's barely touched me in weeks, my vibrator has been my best friend, and now he wants to fuck me. Does murder turn him on?

His hand cupping my breast answers that question. He's twisted. My Guy, the man who saves me from life as a fondle bot for the assholes at the warehouse has lost his ever-loving mind. The feel of his tongue running across my nipple makes me doubt my own sanity since I truly debate whether I can have one last quickie with him before my imminent demise or not. Then I see him: Fred. In our doorway, watching.

"Fred," I say watching Guy's head pop up and stare at me. "Watching."

I can see the anger in his face, then it settles into something I'm not familiar with.

"We can let him watch if you want," he grins.

What the hell? I'm a lady. Does he really think I'm inviting that freaky fucker into our bedroom? At this point I'm doubting my ability to have sex with my own husband due to his murderous ways, but to ask Fred to watch, hell no!

A noise in the hallway halts the creepy, yet hot, scene happening in the bedroom. The hands used to kill my loved ones leave my body, and Guy steps toward the hall to look around. In my mind, I'm cheering him on. Find him. Find him, please.

"It's Fred," I tell him. "Fred moves."

For the briefest second, I think he gets it. Then it's gone. He laughs, shrugs it off, and comes back to the bed. He starts putting the corset on me. He says he wants me to look amazing when everyone comes. I'm sure I will. I always do.

Once I'm dressed, Guy carries me downstairs. I'm barely settled on the couch when a knock comes to the door. I hear the familiar voice of my creator, wannabe father, Bob. Then I hear the answer to problems.

"Where's Petunia?" Sage asks.

I look up as she joins me on the couch. Bob and Guy venture off to look at things out back.

"You look scared," she says.

"Murderer," I tell her then look at the box.

She turns, looks then shakes her head. "You poor thing. They don't understand. They are human. It's okay."

"Fred moves."

Her head cocks to the side as if she's surprised.

"Help me, please."

Sage is my only hope. I just hope Fred doesn't get to her first.

Petunia in a crown

I smile as I pull my tallest ladder back from Petunia's throne. I haven't slept in two days and it's worth it. I can see it now: *She looks regal perched upon the black pedestal that will tell all the world she rules the dollhouse.*

"Wow," Bob says, giving his approval.

"Yeah. You'd never know. It's just perfect."

"What time do people show up?"

"An hour or so."

I think about finding Petunia a coat. While the snow's held off, it can't be over 38 degrees and the temperature is quickly dropping. But I remind myself that I'll be sitting with her on the throne soon enough. When chill seekers and trick or treaters begin to show, I'll climb right up that ladder myself and take my place at my love's side. I can keep her warm. Together, we will watch the world below as Sylvia ringmasters our show.

"You've really created something special here, Guy," Bob says, helping me pull the ladder to the back of the throne so I can climb it later.

"I couldn't have done it without you."

I am nervous about his arrival. He seeing the dolls with their heads twisted off is something I'd been worried about. I don't want him to think I'd ruined his creations. It isn't like I can't put their heads and even limbs back on. But like Fred said he'd be, Bob's impressed. I only hope it's the same for Petunia.

I wave at Marcy, who peeps through the hole again. She's been showing up every hour or so since the final preparations to the backyard began. As soon as she leaves, I'll get Petunia. Generally, when she knows I see her, she gives me a bigger window.

"What's left?" Bob asks.

"Sunset."

"Perfect."

"Oh, by the way, did you bring Fred's dick? The guy's been super helpful. He's most of the reason why this even became a thing. Without his help, it would just have been a little Halloween celebration for me and Petunia. I feel bad about the five inch one—my own insecurities. Isn't cool."

"Sure did. Want me to get it?"

"That would be great," I say, figuring it will be nice for the guy to have his manhood in time for the haunt. *Great for Renee anyway.* "I better go check on Petunia. She still needs make up, and I need to get her on that throne before our favorite peeping, do-good slob comes back."

With that, I leave Bob in the yard to take in the rest of my work. Back in the living room, I smile at my love. "Are you ready, Petunia? I can picture you now. Your throne is ready, and you're going to rock it."

She smiles at me, but something tells me she's not happy.

"Petunia, what's wrong?"

"No Fred."

"For the love of fuck. Do I need to take your voice chip out? I did this for you! Get *off* the Fred kick! He's not leaving! Deal with it. Marcy's even planning to come *with* the church idiots. If you could stop saying that you could even talk to her. For a year now, you've wanted me to show you off. Now's your chance. Why are you ruining it?"

"I'm not," she says, pouting.

"Well, okay then. Let's get your make up on. I need to get you out there before Marcy comes back. The rest of the stage is set. Bob's tinkering with the last few dolls, and I'll have him help Fred with his dick."

Petunia doesn't respond.

"Look, I know you aren't a fan. Hell, probably even Marcy knows that. The entire neighborhood must know how you feel about Fred. But Fred's the reason for this whole event. He even helped me with your throne. Wait until you see it! And think of the cash! Sylvia's script is set and the subscribers are happy to pay $20. Hell, your favorite stalker, 69 or whoever he calls himself, even said he'd pay double. He's even flying in from North Carolina just to get a glimpse of you in real life. You're a star. That's what you wanted! Stalkers and all."

Petunia's are eyes open wide.

"Oh, don't be afraid. You'll be perfectly safe. Your throne is twenty feet up. Besides, I'll be right by your side. I need to find you a coat. First, we've gotta get your crown on."

Twenty minutes later, I push Petunia's chair past the craft store skeleton half buried in the yard. I laugh at the filthy femur, figuring there's no real way to get caught. Even if Marcy brings her dog and the slobbery thing gets to digging by the gazebo, people will just assume the bullies and smelly old decaying Sarah are just props. Fred is brilliant.

"You need help?" Bob calls from the gazebo, where he's managed to straighten the third strobe light that will illuminate a graveyard scene to the left of me and my love's throne.

"Stand in front of the hole."

"The hole?"

I tilt my head in the direction of the fence between Marcy Busy Body's yard and me. Bob smiles, "Gotcha."

When I'm sure his shoulders have any shot she has at a view of us, I hoist Petunia up. "Hang on tight, my love. We have to climb."

In the year I've had Petunia, and ultimately, the rest of the dolls, I've gotten into better shape if I do say so myself. I manage to maneuver the first ten steps or so easily. And, half way up, I'm sure I can safely transport my love to our throne.

When we finally make it to the top, I kiss Petunia on the forehead and straighten her crown. "You're radiant, love. Just like on our wedding day," I say. "Now, I need you to behave. None of this 'Fred' shit. Just be polite and smile at the crowd."

The *idea* of my love doll dressed as a creepy queen corseted and dripping in fake blood is doing something to me. But looking closer at her, I want to *do* something about it. It seems like forever since Petunia and I have spent a quality night together. *Tonight,* I tell myself. Right now, there's work to be done. If we do this right, we will make a fortune.

It'll be a yearly event for me and my love. With Fred's help, we can think of new themes and even advertise more. I can see the crowds now: All of them here to see Petunia and me. *Look at me now, Mom. Try to tell me I don't have a real family now.*

I begin my climb down the ladder, watching Bob and two steps from the top when Petunia shrieks.

"No, Fred, no!" she screams.

The ladder moves. I grip the edge of the throne.

"Jesus, dude, no!" Bob yells out.

I have no idea what's happening as the ladder leaves the throne. All I know is I am about to fall. Panic grips me as I look down on the dollhouse and the magic of it all.

An evil laugh.

Petunia shrieking…

"No Fred!"

"No!"

Petunia is queen

My entire world is unraveling in front of me. I see the panic and the fear in my love's face. I hear the laughter coming from that damn baby dick doll. I can even see Bob rushing forward hoping to help. None of the others see his face though. Fred is staring up at me, his smile twisted into some perverse look of satisfaction at what he is doing. Then it happens. The most horrific thing I can imagine. Fred wins. My Guy, my savior, my love, my everything falls.

I close my eyes, hoping not to see the results of Fred's attack. Maybe if I don't see Guy broken at the bottom of the ladder, it won't really happen. I know that's not how things work, but I can try. Not looking doesn't stop the sounds though. I hear Guy yell as he falls. I also hear my own screams of panic. Then I hear the undoubtable sound of him connecting with the ground. But wait? Wouldn't that be more of thud? What I heard was more solid.

Slowly, I open my eyes. I need to know what's going on despite the fear rushing through me. That's when I see her. Sage. She is by the ladder, already helping Guy to his feet. He's slow. Clearly rattled, possibly injured, but he's alive. Then I see the true carnage, and I'm happy as fuck!

"Sage, what did you do?" Bob asks her as he stares down at Fred on the ground. "Did you push him?"

"Yes. He was trying to hurt Guy. I couldn't stop the fall, but I thought Fred would be a good landing spot, safer than the ground."

Thank God for robot dolls. If she hadn't been here, there would've been nothing I could do to save my husband. If she hadn't been here, no one would've listened to me about Fred. No one would've done anything to stop all this. Sage is my hero. I don't give a damn if she runs on electronics or not.

"I can't believe he did that," I hear Guy mumble. I can imagine how hurt he is to know his best friend tried to kill him. I tried to warn him though. If he'd listened to me or Brenda before he murdered her, none of this would've happened. Stubborn ass man. "How did he do that?" he asks looking over at Bob.

"I thought it would be a cool gift for you. I didn't tell you, wanting it to be a surprise. When I perked Fred up after poker a few months back, I gave him a complete overhaul. He's like Sylvia. They aren't as advanced as Sage, but they are close. I have no idea why he would try to hurt you though or keep his upgrades secret."

"My dollhouse," the twisted remains of Fred mumbles from his place on the ground. "I'm the king."

"That's amazing," Bob smiles as he leans down looking closely at Fred. "Somehow, he got something in his head, decided he wanted it, and tried to take it how he chose. Amazing."

I watch as both my love and Sage turn to look at me. They finally understand. "Petunia knew," Sage tells them. "She told me when we arrived. She told me Fred moves and asked for help."

"That's why you were watching him?" Bob asks then laughs it off. "She's just a doll, Sage. It doesn't work that way. She isn't that smart."

"She's smart enough to know her husband was in trouble. She's also under the illusion that her husband has murdered her entire family by ripping their heads off. Bless her heart."

Okay, she saved my Guy but now she's being a bit of a bitch. I'm the one who says bless your heart. She's stealing my shit. She's also making it sound like I'm sort of a dumbass. She's walking a thin line.

"It makes so much sense now," Guy says running his hands over his face. "Fred suggests I send Busty back. He said Petunia wanted a divorce."

Divorce! That bastard. I wish someone down there would step on his twisted neck again. Hell, maybe Guy should climb up and jump off again to finish the job.

"Divorce isn't in her chip's vocabulary," Sage points out.

"I know. I wasn't thinking. I saw how freaked she was when I took their heads off, but he said she was excited. I let that fucker play me."

"Yes, yes, you did." Sage agrees. "And now you have a front yard full of people waiting to see your dollhouse."

She is right. Worry for my love had made me forget the activities. I wait as Guy gets things finished, and then slowly climbs the ladder again, this time with Bob holding onto the bottom. Once he is beside me, I smile. He starts on about how he was wrong and all that. I don't care. I'm just glad he wasn't hurt.

"My Guy," I tell him as he takes my hand. I hold my head high, ready to welcome the world to our home. Our home, where I'm the queen and my king is human, not a doll with a five-inch dick.

The following day

I am not surprised our dollhouse is such a hit. The neighborhood kids all seem to love it. The church ladies and Marcy can't get enough. They are thrilled to finally meet me and have a bit of conversation. Guy explains to them about my illness and my slow recovery. They don't expect too many words, but you can see they are happy with the few they get. I'm sure I'll be the talk of their next church meeting.

The subscribers are the big deal of the night though. They show up. Some even told Guy they drove for days to get here. Seeing the dollhouse was a dream of theirs. Yes, they are kinky fuckers, but the money we make will pay a lot of bills. Especially all the dough from PetuniaLover69. The little, bald, man who was normally behind the computer screen showed up offering extra money for everything. Can I get a picture with Petunia? Sure, for a hundred bucks. Can I get a picture with Sylvia? Yep, fifty. We even let him have a picture with me kissing his cheek. He paid two-hundred dollars for that one. By the time he and all the others were finished, Guy had a pile of cash and a smile on his face. That is until he remembered about Fred.

Most of the night, he is moping around. Bob and Sage stay in the guest room and even try to help get him in a better mood. It doesn't work. I understand though. I lost Brenda. I know the pain of losing a best friend. I guess that doesn't change even when they try to kill you and take your woman.

"He's sad," I tell Sage as the two of us sit on the couch, watching Guy and Bob in the kitchen talking over a cup of coffee.

"Why?"

"Fred was his friend."

"Ah, I get it," she smiles. "Before Bob upgraded Fred, they were close."

"Even after."

"Fred can be fixed, Petunia. I know it may be hard for you to see him, but it can be done. Bob can limit his abilities, so this doesn't happen again."

I think about it. Sure, he freaks me out. I didn't like him even before the upgrade, but he was or is, whichever, my Guy's best friend. I know what it's like to lose one of those. I don't like the idea of my man hurting.

"Fix Fred," I say with a sigh.

"You're something else, Petunia. I would have sent his remains away. I guess being married makes a difference."

"Love my Guy," I tell her. It is true. Sure, he likes to ignore me when he and Fred had poker nights, and he murdered Brenda then sent her away in a cardboard coffin, but he is my love. I want him happy.

"I'll tell Bob when we leave. It can be a surprise."

I smile at her and watch as she gets up and makes her way to the kitchen. After a few more minutes they say their goodbyes and take off with Fred in his own cardboard coffin. I am not surprised when my love lifts me into his arms after they are gone and carries me up to our room.

Hours later

I lay there in complete bliss as Guy showers after our hours of fun in the bedroom. I suppose a near death experience teaches a human person to experience the good things in life. I may not need my vibrator for a few weeks.

Hearing a noise near the bathroom, I open my eyes expecting to see my man in his full, naked, glory. Instead, Sylvia is standing there, looking toward the open bathroom door. My eyes widen. The golden cunt is NOT seeing my man in the buff.

"Go away," I demand.

She turns her head toward me and then moves toward the bed slowly. "Fred said he would be king of the dollhouse. He said I was to listen to him. Where is he?"

"Dead."

"Who rules the dollhouse now?"

Bless her heart, even with her advanced tech she's a dumb bitch.

"Guy. Guy is king."

"Am I the queen?"

HA! As if bitch. Not in my dollhouse. I think by now they'd learn. That is my man. I will do whatever it takes to make him happy. Even if that means learning new tricks in the bedroom, but I'm not ready for those tricks to include the golden twat just yet. Maybe later, not now.

"No, I'm queen," I tell her. "Guy and Petunia. Our dollhouse."

I watch as she nods her head once, then turns and makes her way out of the bedroom. I wonder where she's going off to. Maybe she needs to get laid. That could be something to do with the spare foot-long dick in the junk drawer downstairs.

"What did you say?" Guy asks as he comes out of the bathroom.

"Guy and Petunia. Our dollhouse," I tell him with a smile.

"Definitely," he laughs.

I wink at him. For now, I'm back to ruling the roost. I knew Freaky Fred wasn't going to win. I have my king, but I'm still the lady of the house, so with a smirk I add, "All hail Queen Petunia."

About the Authors

Erin Lee

USA Today Bestselling Author **Erin Lee**, who also writes as **EL George**, is a dark fiction/reality author and therapist chasing a crazy dream one crazy story at a time. She is the author of *Crazy Like Me*, a novel published in 2015 by Savant Books and Publications, LLC, *Wave to Papa*, 2015, by Limitless Publishing, LLC and *Nine Lives*

(2016). She's also author of *When I'm Dead, Greener, Something Blue, Freak* and *99 Bottles*. She also penned *Losing Faith,* a novella with Black Rose Writing. She is co-author of Black Rose's *The Morning After.* She is also author of the *Diary of a Serial Killer Series* and *Lola, Party of Eight Series* formerly with Zombie Cupcake Press and now home with Crazy Ink, *From Russia, Pretty Bones, Boned, The Ghosts who Raised Me, His Village, Seeds, Resurrection* and *From Russia, With Love.* She is a co-author of the *Moving On Series,* including bestselling *The Ranch* and *Moving On* and *The Cabin.* Other horror and upcoming titles include *Pawn Takes All* and *The Haunt.* Other recent titles include the co-write *Bella Amore* and the award-winning and bestselling six-book *Circus Freak Series.*

Lee is the founder of Crazy Ink Publishing, a multi genre publisher specializing in multi-genre anthologies for all kinds of crazy. Through this venture, she hopes to give readers and authors alike a taste of other realities and worlds so that they can escape into the words.

Lee holds a master's degree in psychology and works with at-risk families and as a court appointed special advocate. When she isn't busy dissecting the human experience, she enjoys escaping from reality through reading and spending time with her muses and canine freak show companions and therapy dogs – Thomas the Terrier and Milo Muse.

To learn more about Lee's work, visit www.authorerinlee.com or www.crazyink.org or take a look at her Facebook author page by visiting www.facebook.com/gonecrazytalksoon.

To join her Facebook street team and fan club group, look for the Crazy Inklings group. Warning: It's a madhouse in there… www.facebook.com/CrazyInklings

Rena Marin

International Bestselling Author **Rena Marin** was born in a small town in East Tennessee where she, her husband Daniel, and two children-- Cody and Amber--still reside today.

Growing up, reading and writing her own stories was Rena's favorite pastime. Her once-unreachable dream of becoming a published writer came true when she was in high school and found herself with many writing awards and accolades, including a short story in *Reader's Digest.*

After starting her own business, Rena continued writing shorts online before moving on to freelance work. Taking a chance, she and a friend submitted a novel to their first publishing company and were delighted to be accepted.

As a member of Crazy Ink Publishing, Rena now has several co-written series underway, including the Best-Selling *Dead Oak Terrors Series.* *Halloween Nightmare*, the first book in that series, recently won the Reality Bites Best Horror Book of 2018. Rena also has her own solo series called The *Witches of Dark Hollow Ridge* and will be releasing more solo projects throughout 2019 as an exclusive author for Crazy Ink. She looks forward to bringing readers with her into a world of magic and adventure.

Keeping close to her short story roots, Rena is part of several anthologies with many more in the works.

A lover of all forms of entertainment, Rena enjoys horror and fantasy movies new and old. When she isn't writing or working, she often finds herself cuddled on the couch with her family—including their five fur babies—and lost in a fantasy world or hoping to be scared.

To learn more about Main's work, visit:

https://renamarinauthor.wixsite.com/website or

follow her on Facebook at

www.facebook.com/AuthorRenaMarin/

Find out where the adventure began!

A twisted romance
Petunia
INTERNATIONAL BESTSELLING AUTHORS
ERIN LEE
RENA MARIN

Petunia's arrival

There are dudes who will go a whole lifetime without true love. They'll live alone in big houses like mine and pass the time drinking beers alone at night with a bottle of lotion and never enough Kleenex; always anxious for Thursday night poker with the guys. They'll work nine to five and pretend they use their Planet Fitness memberships just for a shot at the disinterested big-titted blonde at the counter who checks folks in. They'll take it as a sign of hope when she waves at them and tells them to have a good day without even looking up from her phone. They're the ones who are sick—not me.

I've waited my whole life for my girl too. But not anymore and not like them. *Fuck you, Sarah.* Every dime I've saved and matching tea cloth I've bought has been for Petunia. That's her name—after the flowers I planted for her outside our front porch. She's bound to love them. They're beautiful like her. Even Marcy Brown—the nosey neighbor next door who peeks at me through the purposely shaggy shrubs—commented on them.

I'm not stupid, you see. I've been studying women and what they want my whole life for this moment. I even minored in human anatomy just to be sure I knew what I was doing when I finally met the girl of my dreams.

It's hard to believe she's finally coming home to me. I try not to think about it as I pull the garlic from the cupboard. On second thought, and remembering what my mother always said about mints on a first date, I put it back and instead reach for the pepper. I want to believe that Petunia wouldn't mind garlic breath, but I'm also not too sure of that. I mean, like they say, first impressions are everything and Sarah hated it.

I pull the roast from the fridge. I curse myself for forgetting to clean it. I'll have to ask her to wait for me at the dining room table. If she sees the grime on the freezer drawer, she might think I'm a pig. I'm really not. I just haven't had much use for cleaning.

I've spent months bringing the place into spit shine shape. I even vacuumed just last week between the couch cushions. I can't wait to snuggle up with my girl to watch TV. Never again will it be just me laughing at *Saturday Night Live* or rooting for those gold miners.

Peeling off the taut, store packaged shrink wrap, I tell myself not to think of her. I can't stand the idea that—right now—breathing must be so hard for her. *Hang in there, love. You're almost home. Never again will either of us be alone.*

It's a promise I intend to keep. Obviously, there will be errands and things that will keep us apart, but that's no big thing. Even ordinary couples separate on weekends to grocery shop. My Petunia won't have to miss me long. I've made sure of it. I've arranged for everything. Aside from the random and rare family obligation, I don't intend for either of us to leave the house.

With three years of consulting jobs lined up, I can't see either us needing much outside our home. And what a marvelous home I've made for us! From Grandma's refinished front foyer, up the winding oak staircase and straight through to the attic, I cannot wait to give my girl a tour. One room at a time, I'll show my love around. I've even saved the last one—a room in the basement but not near the furnace room that I figure she can use for crafts—up to her. Secretly, I hope she picks lavender to match the flowers I've planted for her. But I will paint those walls any color she wants. There's really no limit to what I'd do for my Petunia. I would have done it for Sarah.

I stab the slab of meat over and over, watching the fork sink into the raw carcass. Blood seeps from the holes and drips onto the granite counter. Unable to help it, I reach down and with my pointer finger, swipe up a swab of blood.

Bringing it to my mouth, I inhale the copper smell. Then, I let my tongue swirl around the metallic tang of cow blood. I tell myself it's the last time. Petunia is a proper girl. She won't like me playing with food.

It's true. There will be some things I have to give up. But that's what marriage is: compromise. For two months, I've practiced putting the seat down and always replenished the empty toilet paper roll. I've even walked my socks to the laundry basket. I hope Petunia somehow knows what a wonderful husband I'll be. With two weeks to our wedding, she has to be wondering.

But wondering isn't for me. A wave of anticipation washes over me as I plop the bloody meat into the crock pot. It occurs to me that people don't believe a person's life can be changed—I mean fully—in an instant. They are wrong. The death of a loved one, a broken heart. Those things can change everything. For me, the change comes with Petunia.

After I manage to stuff the crock pot with carrots, potatoes, and a dash of salt, I move to the sink to wash my hands. Inspecting my nails, I'm pleased to see the manicure has paid off. My large hands no longer carry the calluses that once came from hard work.

It's been three years. Since leaving that dead end contracting job and starting the consulting work, everything's changed. The guys at work told me I was crazy when I first walked off the job site. But they were cowards. Cowards never face their fears. Instead, they hide in the dark pretending they aren't passionate about anything.

Roy Shay was like that. The only thing that man was passionate about was the bottle. I won't miss poker nights, the only thing that remained of that job site or any of it until now. Now, Thursdays will be for me and Petunia. We'll even call them date nights if she agrees. I picture her looking at me with a crooked smile and sparkling eyes as I surprise her week after week with new activities. Oh, we have so much to look forward to!

I move quickly through the kitchen, down a long hallway, and finally to the foyer where the heart of a majestic staircase welcomes me. I take the stairs two at a time before finally making my way three doors down to the master bedroom. There, I peel my T-shirt over my head and turn to the closet. It's the last time I'll ever undress alone. In a peculiar way, it almost feels like a house of cards is about to come tumbling down. I can't imagine how Petunia feels.

They say true love comes when you least expect it. In a funny way, that's exactly what happened. I am just about to step into my final shower as a bachelor when the doorbell rings. Scurrying to answer, I never even bother to put on my shirt. Instead, I grab a set of white, plastic gloves and my black hoodie from the top of my dresser and run as quickly as I can to the stairs.

"Coming!" I yell, pulling on the gloves and then the hoodie. "Be right there!" There's no way I'm missing Petunia's arrival.

Finally, and panting, I pull open the door. A bald man in a brown uniform sighs and pushes out a clipboard and pen.

"Please sign."

I have no time for small talk. For once, I'm grateful for his rudeness. I sign the slip as fast as I can and wait for him to move aside. There, on my front porch, is the box I've waited for.

It's nearly six feet long: bigger than I thought. I wait for the man to get into his delivery truck. When he does, and with a quick glance toward my and Marcy's shared shrubs, I bend down. I pull in a long, deep breath through my nose as I move my face only inches from the cardboard box marked "fragile" and "this side up."

The smell of petunias invades my nostrils. It's so strong I almost wonder if they covered her in perfume. I hope not. Petunia's not that kind of girl.

She's more like the girl next door. Too anxious to rescue her, and confident enough that Marcy's at choir practice, I grip both sides of the box with my gloved hands. Pulling—hard—I heave the box inside and wonder how it could be that the box weighs this much. The thing has to weigh two hundred pounds.

I suppose I'll find out soon enough. In long, determined huffs and pulls, I manage to slide the box into the house without any obvious damage. Red duct tape that lines one corner has me concerned. What if the contents are damaged?

"Hang on, love!"

It takes a good ten minutes to finally get the box to my grandmother's old 70's style olive green, velvet couch. I lay the box parallel to the base of the couch and head into the kitchen for a knife. This isn't exactly how I planned it. But then, can you ever really plan true love?

Petunia's journey

I never knew I hated the dark this much. I suppose I should've expected it though. Being locked away, alone, waiting to meet the man of your dreams is a lonely, dark experience. The driver hadn't been much help either. Apparently, he didn't realize just how important my first impression was. I want to look great, show the one who's been waiting on me exactly what he's getting. Instead, I've been bounced around in this truck like some bag of garbage on the way to the dump. How is that fair? Doesn't he know the meaning of the word "fragile?"

That's me, you know, fragile. Always alone, waiting for it to be my turn. Until now, I'd watched in silence as life happened around me. No one ever cared enough to make me part of it. No, instead, I just lingered, waiting for the right man, or even woman if that was the case, to finally make me whole. It is finally happening now though. This is it. This is my chance at happiness.

When I was told it was my turn to start my happily ever after, I was surprised. I still remember the voices talking to one another about the "poor sap" that had given them a call. I was so angry they would refer to him—the man for me—that way. He was no sap. He's *my* man.

"He saw that she was available online," one had laughed like it was the funniest thing he'd heard all day.

I didn't appreciate his tone.

"Yeah, he's decided he wants Petunia," the other added while holding his fat belly and bending over in his amusement.

I wondered, what was so funny? They didn't see it. Why couldn't they see just how perfect my situation was? I was chosen. My life would finally start. I didn't know the name of the man who'd chosen me, the asses never said it. I wish they had. The moment I found out about him, my excitement began to grow. I know he's going to like me~that's not an issue. The only thing I do wonder about is will he love me? Will I be enough to make him happy?

Leaving the place I'd formerly called home didn't bother me. I thought I'd be a bit upset like the other girls had been. I mean, the fulfillment center was where it all happened. The cold, busy warehouse was where I became me. It didn't matter though. Home was where your love was. And now I was heading to it.

The guys who'd wandered around my first home were perverts and assholes. They liked to touch me, knowing I couldn't stop them. They'd squeeze a tit here and slap my ass there, like it was funny. I suppose they were hard up. They didn't understand what love was or that I was intended for someone else. I always knew that. The man waiting on me would never do those kinds of things to me. I know he'll be the perfect gentleman.

When it was time to leave, their hands were everywhere. I know, I know, they had to do it, but still, no one should touch me but the one I'm destined for. I'm allowed to dream, right? Instead, I was tossed around like I was nothing special. That's not true though. I am special. I'm chosen.

Lying on my back, staring up at the nothingness above, I can't help but imagine my new home. I wonder if it's a two-story house. When the television in the corner of the fulfillment center played, most of the shows had two-story homes. I don't know much about architecture or style, but the idea of sitting in the upstairs bedroom, looking down on a gorgeous lawn with the man I love at my side is a dream come true. It would be for any girl.

Oh, our yard. I hope we have a big one. Lots of space for flowers, maybe a fountain of some kind, or even a gazebo. Those seem so romantic on the movies the late-night guy used to watch while he sat in the corner, fondling himself when he was the only one working. I can already imagine myself out there enjoying the sunshine and curled up in the gazebo while my man cuts the grass. A slight summer breeze blowing in my hair will make me even more appealing to him as I offer him a wink and a wave. The grass will have to wait, I'm sure. How could he resist me beckoning to him like that?

I've already decided I'm going to be the perfect girlfriend. I hope he'll make me his bride soon. I don't want to be one of those girls that lives with a guy for ages, but he never commits. No, I want a ring on my finger. I want to be official. I'll do everything the perfect wife is supposed to. I'll cook. I'll clean. I'll keep him satisfied. We'll talk about our days, share our nights, and even talk about our dreams. I know he's a dreamer. He has to be. We're going to have so much in common.

Feeling a bump, then a sudden stop, I open my eyes again to the darkness around me. *Is this it? Am I home?* When they closed the box back at the factory, I didn't care too much. Sure, I hated the idea of being packed away in the dark, alone, but leaving didn't faze me one bit. I didn't do the one last look thing. I didn't feel as though I should say goodbye. Nah, it was more like good riddance to the jacking-off-night-guy. Adios to the pervs who worked during the day that liked to fondle me and say "catch you later, doll" to the chick that answered the phones and shook her head each time an order came through.

When the truck didn't start moving again, I knew we'd arrived. I was finally home. I would see him—my perfect man—soon. I hated not being able to see what was happening. The only sliver of light that had been granted to me had been quickly covered before they loaded me into the truck. The sound of duct tape told me they were ensuring no damage took place during my trip. In a way, that was sweet I suppose. It was the one last gesture those assholes offered before sending me out into the world.

The sound of the truck opening told me the driver was coming. I didn't know how he would get me home. Would he carry me? That's how a true lady should be treated, you know. Carried to the threshold of her new home and into the waiting arms of her soon-to-be husband. I knew better in this case though. When the delivery guy arrived, my box was still open. I saw him dropping ashes all over the floor from the cigarette hanging in his mouth while he eyed all the merchandise in the warehouse. He was probably wondering if he should make an order himself. He didn't strike me as the kind that could find a great girl like me on his own.

When the box lurched, I froze. The last thing I needed was to be injured before I made it to my destination. No, I wanted to be perfect. I wish they'd clothed me though. I didn't want my new boyfriend to think that I was easy. I doubt he'll see it that way though. He will understand. Those people aren't like us. They didn't care what I looked like when they packed me away. No, they were just wanting me gone. If I'd had my way, I'd have been wearing a beautiful lavender dress with matching high heels. My hair would've been in place. My head would have been attached, and I'd be looking like one of those models on the television. My green eyes would be sparkling, and my excitement would be etched upon my face. Instead, I am lying in a cardboard box, naked and hairless.

The plastic wrapped around me stifled my breathing some but wasn't going to kill me. Still, the idea of fresh air was welcome. Speaking of, I'd never truly had fresh air. I lived in a factory. That would be something else I could experience for the first time with him: Sharing a forever home.

Him. I couldn't wait to meet him. I didn't want to hide away from the darkness inside the box any longer. Instead, I wanted to see everything. I wanted to see his face the first time he saw me. It would be something I remembered forever. Our first look, our first touch, our first meeting. It would be magical.

The driver dropped me hard, the bastard. Then, I heard what sounded like a doorbell ring. This was it. It was finally happening. The moments seemed to be crawling by, and then I heard it.

"Coming." It was him. It had to be. He was on his way to take me out of the grasp of this rude stranger that didn't care that I was fragile.

"Sign here," the familiar voice of the driver announced. I noticed the tone. He was judging my man. I was right. He is a bastard. "All yours," he mumbled, his words barely audible. He had to be walking away.

I heard a soft grunt as I began to move again. Bless his heart, the packaging was making me heavier than normal. I wish he didn't have to struggle like this. I wanted to reassure him that I wasn't really this big. He'd see that when he threw open the box though. He'd see my curves and know I was worth the wait.

Speaking of waiting, the longer it took him to slide my box across the floor, the more anxious I became. I also cussed the guys at the warehouse even more. Those assholes knew how difficult it would be for him to maneuver the box they put me in. Would it have killed them to make things a bit easier? Being wrapped in plastic was bad enough but all the packing that was stuffed around me was too confining. I felt like I was trapped. I didn't have to worry though; he was out there now. I was in our new home and he was working tirelessly to free me. I couldn't stand the suspense. Soon I would see our home and him. The man who'd been waiting for me. The man who'd chosen to be with only me.

A scraping sound took me by surprise. "Careful, love," I called out, knowing that he would hear me. The rest of the world may not understand me, but I had no doubts he would. He was special.

Suddenly, the box lid raised, letting the soft light flow inside. This was it. I would finally see my new life. Through the plastic, I peered, taking in the colors around me. I saw olive green almost immediately. From my distorted view, I imagined it had to be a couch. There was no way he had me in a chair. I was still lying flat and was far too tall for that. Beside the sofa, whose olive color I adored, was a side table. The lamp perched on top seemed to drip with crystals that were catching the rays of sunlight and cascading them around the room. It had to be expensive. My man had seen to me only having the best.

I wanted to see things clearly. In my mind, I was rushing him to remove the plastic and let me look around. That would take time though. He was busy unzipping the bag that surrounded the rest of my body. Once the bag was free, I could feel his hands against my skin.

What was that? Gloves? Why would my love need to use gloves to touch me? Then, it struck me. He was being careful. He wanted to make sure he didn't hurt me. How sweet is that?

I waited while he lifted my body from the box. He wasn't like the others. Not once did he grab me in the wrong way or stare too long at my sweetest parts. No, he was moving me gingerly, taking care not to hurt me in any way. That was another sign that this was meant to be. We were meant to be. He understood that I was a lady.

Through my blurred view, I saw him moving closer. It was finally time. Slowly, he lifted my head, holding me close to his chest while he carefully removed the plastic.

"Now you can breathe, love."

His precious words echoed in my ears. *He called me love.* I was already important to him.

The plastic fell free. Finally. "Let me see you," I whispered as he slowly pulled me away from his chest where he'd been caressing me. That's when it happened. That was the moment I saw my fate. He stared down at me with love in his dark eyes. His head was hidden by the hoodie he wore, but I didn't care about his hair. It didn't matter if he was bald, blond, or even gray. In my eyes, he was perfect. In my eyes, he was mine. All mine.

www.ingramcontent.com/pod-product-compliance
Lightning Source LLC
Chambersburg PA
CBHW071423150726
48000CB00001B/452